CITY DOC TO THE RESCUE

KRISTINE LYNN

MEDICAL ROMANCE

Recycling programs for this product may not exist in your area.

ISBN-13: 978-1-335-99380-9

City Doc to the Rescue

For questions and comments about the quality of this book, please contact us at CustomerService@Harlequin.com.

Harlequin Enterprises ULC
22 Adelaide St. West, 41st Floor
Toronto, Ontario M5H 4E3, Canada
www.Harlequin.com

HarperCollins Publishers
Macken House, 39/40 Mayor Street Upper,
Dublin 1, D01 C9W8, Ireland
www.HarperCollins.com

Printed in U.S.A.

1 2 3 4 5 6 7 8 9 10 HDC 28 27 26 25

A brand-new trilogy from Kristine Lynn!

High Altitude Docs

You've reached the peak of medicine...

Welcome to Washington's Olympic Mountains, where the extreme terrain attracts the most fearless climbers—and the most daredevil docs!

Mountain medic Erin plans to take emergency medicine in the region to even greater heights... *if* she can convince city doc Reese to sign off on it. Will a week stranded in the wilderness win him over?

Surgeon brothers Ian and Greg have escaped their city lifestyles looking for adventure and find it working at Erin and Reese's new state-of-the-art medical facility. As new medical personnel arrive on the scene—and on their minds!—Greg and Ian wonder if they're in for the adventure of a lifetime...

Find out where it all began in Reese and Erin's story
City Doc to the Rescue
Available now!

And their legacy continues
with Ian's and Greg's stories

Coming soon!

Dear Reader,

Welcome to book one of High Altitude Docs! I am enamored with the Pacific Northwest—rugged mountain peaks, wild animals and raging seas are all in my backyard!

I wanted to explore two characters with different capacities for risk set against a rugged backcountry backdrop.

Erin, a backcountry EMT, grew up in the Olympic Mountains. Helping people learn how to play in them safely is important to her. With a city doc, Reese, deciding if her clinic gets built, she worries it's doomed. Reese doesn't take risks and she's all about them—physically at least. It's a different story when her heart is on the line, though.

A helicopter crash shows us through these characters that risk is a part of life, but love will always be the riskiest venture of all. It's also always worth it, as we learn in this forced-proximity, fish-out-of-water, opposites-attract story.

Thanks for joining me as I introduce two new lovebirds looking for a chance to safely explore love and all its joys.

I look forward to your thoughts on how their path to love unfolds. Contact me on Instagram or Facebook, or by email at kristinelynnauthor@gmail.com.

Thanks for reading!

XO, *Kristine*

Hopelessly addicted to espresso and HEAs, **Kristine Lynn** pens high-stakes romances in the wee morning hours before teaching writing at an Oregon college. Luckily,, the stakes there aren't as dire. When she's not grading, writing, or searching for the perfect vanilla latte, she can be found on the hiking trails behind her home with her daughter and puppy. She'd love to connect on X, Facebook or Instagram.

Books by Kristine Lynn

Harlequin Medical Romance

Royal York Hospital

Wedding Date with Dr. Petrides

Paging Dr. Morrison

Doctor's Nine-Month Rival

Brought Together by His Baby
Accidentally Dating His Boss
Their Six-Month Marriage Ruse
A Kiss with the Irish Surgeon
Nine Months to Marry the Princess
How to Resist Your Enemy

Visit the Author Profile page at Harlequin.com.

For Bev Scholfield. Why would she lie?

Also for Brenda, Katie, Kristina and Nat. Our salt-laced mornings and late whiskey nights have built a feral family out of five independent women. Here's to deeper swimming holes, better waves and sunnier skies. Oh, and men with fully functioning kitchens and prefrontal cortexes.

CHAPTER ONE

ERIN WALLACE STORMED out of the meeting, her fists clenched tight at her sides.

"If he thinks he can just—"

"He can change the schedule if he needs because he's the money," her boss, Lila, said in a singsong voice from the front office of the Hoodsport emergency-medical-services outpost.

She'd been singing the same refrain for weeks now, ever since Erin sent yet another assessment to Seattle Memorial Hospital asking them to consider a fully functioning clinic in Hoodsport. They had too many injuries coming off Hurricane Ridge and the other peaks in the Olympic Mountains—not to mention water injuries from people fishing in the Hood Canal. Getting them to Seattle Memorial was too risky by flight, thanks to the wet, cold Pacific Northwest weather that sat over their state most of the year.

Seattle's answer? Send an annoying, overcommunicative suit to survey the EMS outpost and proposed area of impact for himself. On one of the three flyable days of the year, when, of course, he wouldn't see the need for the program Erin had proposed. Oh, and before he arrived, could Erin please take care of the following checklist?

Have a recent risk assessment done for the month of August?

Bring in the staff so he could take interviews on the most egregious cases?

Prepare a short tour of the area so he could survey the greatest areas of need? This one had a caveat—nothing too risky. Ha! Did the guy know where he was coming to visit? Their parking lot had a black-bear mother and cub that visited each morning. Risk was the name of the game out there, no matter where they went.

Never mind that Erin had completed the whole checklist in July for this guy's predecessor, who'd never showed. Couldn't they share information?

"You want this program, you gotta play ball. Do I need to remind you about the hiker from last month? Mike?"

Erin groaned. The EMS field supervisor wasn't wrong, but still.

"No. I don't think I'll ever forget that." Mike had fallen thirty-two feet off a rock face and the EMTs had carried him down the path since the flight team didn't have anywhere to land. He'd have been fine if they'd arrived in Hoodsport to medical services, but there was only so much the ambulance could do. Mike hadn't made it halfway around the drivable pass before he'd succumbed to his injuries. The worst part was, there were at least ten other scenarios like that each year. "It's not like I don't know why we're doing this. But could he make it any more difficult for us?"

Just in case he could, she knocked on wood. Out there in the Washington wilderness, it paid to be a little superstitious.

"Probably. But I look forward to watching you tame or scare him off, either way." Lila smiled as she restocked the gauze and other dry supplies. Then, she grew uncharacteristically serious. "Erin, you've watched too much happen here to let this guy get the best of you. You know what we need and how to get it. So go get it."

Erin nodded, even though inside she felt a rare combination of nerves and annoyance.

"Fine," she said, relenting.

This was so unfair. She was supposed to be using one of her rare days off—and a sunny one, at that—to hike the South Fork Skokomish River Trail, and instead she was playing babysitter to a hospital suit.

So. Unfair.

"I'm putting on the coffee. I'm going to need a vat of it today if I'm going to survive the whole day with that insufferable, stubborn greenhorn—"

"Guy responsible for giving us hospital money," Lila reminded her.

"Yeah, him." Erin hit Brew on the coffee maker and sat down with a huff. Maybe she'd take him up the South Fork as part of her tour. It would serve him right for ruining the one clear day they'd had in a month—a day when Erin wasn't even on the ambulance rig. "When does he get here?" she asked Lila.

Thankfully, Lila was the kind of boss that was more like a friend, even though the field supervisor was a decade older. There was something intimate about life in a small town, especially a mountain-range town that had the kind of adventure seekers who chose to live here year-round.

"Around noon."

Erin glanced at her watch. It was only nine twenty and her list was done. She could take a short jaunt up the pass to see what was coming in, which was the only real way to tell the weather out there. It could change on a dime. Hell, she might even still have time for a quick catnap, since she hadn't slept the night before.

She'd been too anxious about his arrival and the new "checklist" he'd included. This mattered to her, and for more than just the care of her town, and the visitors that made it their landing spot for adventure each year.

Her dad needed this as much as she did.

Her phone chimed as she gathered her keys and hat to head to the ridge. Speak of the devil. She couldn't help but smile, a pretty recent development when her dad called.

"Hey, there, Dad. I was just thinking about you." The cough that came through the line activated a ping of worry in her already frayed nerves. "How you feeling?"

"Oh, fine. Fine. Just calling to see if you're heading to the fork today and if you want some company."

Erin shut her eyes. Her dad was always up for adventure, which had been a barrier to their closeness during Erin's youth. It had meant he chased "the rush" instead of being the stability she'd needed as a child and teen under his sole care.

Now, though, she saw his appreciation for that kind of high that only came with her drug of choice—the right cocktail of risk and adrenaline. The Olympic Range and Hood Canal gave her both, and with some experience and age in her favor, she had her dad to thank for giving her access to the things that sustained her when the rest of life got too hard.

That wasn't to say they had the perfect relationship or anything, just that she'd started to see things from a more nuanced point of view. Him finding out he had acute emphysema helped bridge that gap.

"I wish I could take you with me," she lied. Sure, she wished he could go, but he'd become a liability with his illness. He needed treatment or he'd… She didn't want to think about it. Suffice it to say, the clinic's proposed oxygen hyperbaric chamber would help her father's condition as much as it would hikers with altitude sickness. "But I've got a suit from Seattle coming in to take a look at what we're asking for and he'll be here at lunch. I'm gonna make a quick run up the pass to check on the weather, then I'm afraid I'm out for the day. Can I swing by and bring you dinner when I'm done?"

"Sounds good, hun. And good luck out there."

"Thanks, Dad," she said, ending the call. She grabbed her day sack and headed out the door. She'd need all the luck she could get.

Erin was out of breath when she got to the top of the ridge, but it looked good from what she could tell. Some building cumulonimbus on the horizon by the south range, but unless the winds shifted, they'd be fine wherever she took The Suit. She jogged down, her thumbs hooked in the straps of her pack to keep it flush with her back.

The view was majestic, the lupine and aster dappling the hills in color. She loved her hometown, even if it sometimes felt like a prison. A snow-capped, mountain-ringed, flower-infested paradise of a prison, but still. If she'd just gone to medical school, she wouldn't have to beg some guy who couldn't care less for what was obviously a need. She could open a clinic on her own, but no. As an EMT she didn't have the same privileges as a physician or surgeon. Which made her think about how she'd gotten to that point.

Dad.

It wasn't his current illness that had driven her to getting her EMT qualification, but rather the way she'd grown up with a risk taker at the helm of their family.

How many bones had he broken the year Erin's

mom left them? Six? Each one had meant a lengthy hospital stay that led to an even lengthier recovery. She'd been, what? Eight years old? And had to care for her dad by doing the chores and taking herself to school each day. All because the only thing he couldn't say no to was the call of the mountains.

Medical school might have been the goal at one point, but how could she consider it when she'd be going at it alone? Alone and caring for a perpetually injured parent? Nah, it was easier to get her EMT certification, so she could start bringing in an income and learn how to help her dad with his myriad injuries.

So at eighteen, that's what she'd done, and hadn't looked back since. Experience in the PNW told her that looking back was a surefire way to trip herself up.

When Erin got off the ridge, it was still early. She grabbed a breakfast sandwich from Mo's, and threw it in her pack, along with an energy drink and some trail mix for later.

She jogged back to the outpost instead of her small cabin, which was behind it. This way, she could catch a few minutes of shut-eye on the cots they kept there for overnight shifts and then get up and run the numbers again before The Suit came.

It wasn't the ideal day off, but at least the morning had been hers. She snuggled into a hoodie she kept at the station and pulled her phone out to spy on The Suit's social media. What was his name again? Ritchie Valens? No, that was the singer. She tried a few variations and then put the phone down beside her.

That's how she found herself sometime later, when a swift kick to the thigh woke her from the deepest sleep she'd had in months.

"I'm up," she said, shooting to her feet. Her Hoodsport EMT hoodie was half up her torso, and she had moisture pooled in one corner of her lips. She wiped it and gave Lila—the source of the kick, she now saw—a sheepish grin. "Wow. I must not have set an alarm. When does The Suit get here? I need to rinse off before I have to deal with him and his ridiculous requests."

Lila coughed. Erin gave her a pat on the shoulder.

"You okay?" Erin asked.

Lila's eyes bulged. She cleared her throat and gestured with her chin to whatever was behind Erin.

Erin figured it out a minute too late, as per usual.

"Oh." She straightened her shirt, wiped her mouth again, as well as under her eyes this time, since she was pretty sure she was still boasting mascara from the time she'd spent in Sailor Jennie's last night. She tried to tame her strawlike blond mop atop her head, but nothing short of a salon that specialized in exorcisms was going to help.

Not that it mattered. She turned around slowly, her hands tucked in her jean short pockets. Sure enough, The Suit was there, his own hands tapping what appeared to be biceps that were in the running for the cover of Hunky Hospital Guys calendars, if those things existed.

Not that the man himself was any less attractive, or in a suit, she realized. He was actually alarmingly cute in his own Seattle Memorial polo and REI hiking pants.

Ugh. Why am I in jean shorts and a work T-shirt? At the least, she'd have wanted to put on an ambulance quarter-zip fleece and some Fjällräven hiking pants.

"Hi," Erin said. She gave an embarrassed wave and bit her bottom lip. "I'm Erin Wallace, lead emergency medical technician here at Hoodsport EMS. Nice to meet you."

The Seattle Suit/hunk regarded her from under slitted eyes. No smile. Great. There went any luck or positive energy she needed to succeed with her pitch.

Finally, he held out a hand.

"I'm Dr. Reese Vallen, The Suit. And whether it's nice to meet you or not remains to be seen."

CHAPTER TWO

REESE VALLEN WASN'T sure whether to laugh at the woman in front of him, or give her a piece of his mind. She'd been rude, was clearly unprepared, and her whole demeanor was sloppy.

Her hands sat on her hips, and somehow, despite her disheveled appearance, confidence wafted off her. For a split second, he was… He was jealous.

Well, that's weird. Why would he be jealous of a woman who looked like she'd just come off three weeks of an expedition? And who snapped about him the same way his ex, Jack-Lynn, did about every little thing.

Because she also doesn't look like much fazes her. And everything fazed Reese, or had since the death of his sister, Allie, and his wife's departure from his life just a year later.

"I'm the first to admit when I've made a mistake, and clearly, I have. I ran up the ridge to see where I'd like to take you and what the weather will do, and took a nap while I waited. If you're able to give me five minutes to get my bearings, I'll make sure this trip is worth your time."

He wasn't sure five minutes would change anything. She didn't seem to be taking him—or this—seriously.

And yet… The way she'd bit her bottom lip, as if she'd been mortified at the way he'd found her. It was disarming and sneaked into his chest, forcing something foreign up his throat and out of his mouth before he could react as he'd been rewired by Jack-Lynn to do. Namely, defend himself and call this woman out on…well, everything.

But somehow, being around Erin brought the old Reese back, the one that hadn't minded a little adventure now and then.

"Let's take ten and meet back here? We've got a long day ahead of us, but I know what it's like to be caught with my pants down, so to speak."

She nodded, and before she turned away, a hint of color flashed on her cheeks.

Lila, the field supervisor, brought him a steaming cup of coffee. Despite the fact that the weather was warm for the Pacific Northwest this time of year, the cup still felt good in his hands. He'd been on edge already making this trip, and the woman who was supposed to be leading them had undone his defenses even more. Not because of her appearance, or not the rough edge of it, anyway.

But because she actually looked as if she belonged up here. Her tanned, toned legs said the jaunt she'd taken "up the ridge"—whatever that meant—was a regular thing for her. He glanced in the back as she gathered supplies, and her easy way of moving around this rugged medical space added to the effect.

He didn't hike, didn't go into whatever she'd deemed backcountry. No one in his family did, not after Allie had died. He shivered in spite of the heat from the coffee in his hands. Sure, that had been in a skiing accident, but the way he saw it, both required the same amount of risk for not a lot of reward.

Was losing her life worth the ten-minute high of barreling down a slope? He'd never get the chance to ask her. He should have gone with her that day when she'd asked. Or should have told her no—the weather was too variable. But he'd done nothing instead. Just sat at home fighting with his wife about something he couldn't recall all these years later.

And that singular mistake haunted each decision he made, every day after. Including Jack-Lynn walking out on him.

"Cream and sugar are on the back table," Lila told him. He added two sugars and a dose of cream, and took a sip. While he normally didn't drink coffee he didn't make, this was actually pretty good. He must have shown his surprise because Lila added, "Courtesy of Erin. She makes a mean cup of coffee, even roasts the beans herself. Little side hobby, as if the girl didn't have enough on her plate trying to save the planet and her family with it."

"It's good," he said. And meant it. What he didn't ask? Who *was* Erin? What drove her? Because so far, the woman who'd sent him the most thorough report he'd ever seen, one not written by a clinical research physician, was incongruous with the half-put-together one he'd just met.

"If you want more, make yourself at home." Lila excused herself. "I've got to get the ambulance ready for its shift."

While he waited for Erin, he perused the photos on the wall behind the couch. They seemed to be a series of the medics at the outpost with a civilian. Some had been taken at the hospital, others at the outpost. A select few were back outside, on the top of one peak or another.

There were hundreds. Many of them were with Erin at various ages.

"They're the people we rescued. The ones who survive." Erin appeared at his side.

The ones who survive. He held his coffee tighter. How many would be on the other wall? The one boasting numbers no one wanted to highlight?

The numbers she might have the ability to fix. Maybe. It's not as if he didn't know the statistics. Every year around three recreational tourists—backpackers, climbers, mountaineers—lost their lives in the park. Was that worth the start-up costs of a whole new clinic? He'd come to the outpost because his predecessor had warned what would happen if he didn't.

Erin Wallace was relentless and would come to him if he didn't.

That didn't make him any more inclined to say yes to the proposal she'd outlined. It wasn't as if he wanted to say no. With an unlimited budget and staff to support the project, it was probably a good one—to have a major hospital cover the liability and overhead of a rural clinic was actually a brilliant model, if for no other reason than it made sure the patients had continuity of care.

But they weren't working with an unlimited budget. Or staff. Who in their right mind would come all the way out here to run a remote clinic?

"They go back up?" he asked, pointing to what looked like a father-son duo on a mountaintop. "I mean, they heal and put themselves right back in harm's way?" This particular photo had the pair posing with Erin and another man—her boyfriend? He ignored the thin slice of jealousy that nicked his heart. It wasn't—couldn't be—aimed at the mystery man for the way his arm was slung casually around Erin's shoulder, her head resting on his chest. It was more likely a result of seeing what he could never have…

Getting to be in a photo with a stunning woman with an equally stunning backdrop wasn't in the cards for him. Neither part of it.

What he'd learned? That risk wasn't just a physical thing someone took on. It had to do with the emotional peaks people put themselves on as well. Love was, in his experience, the greatest risk of all.

If he hadn't loved Allie as much as he had, or Jack-Lynn…their losses would have been manageable. But it was love that had crippled him.

So it was simple. Aside from the one person—

the most important one, at that—left in his life, he wasn't going to let love in ever again.

"They don't see it that way. The people who choose to go back into the wilderness are reclaiming their power, not letting the hard thing that shaped them also take away their spirit. You have to understand that, right?"

He couldn't understand that, no. In his estimation, it was better to have a life—with a functioning body and mind—than a "fulfilled spirit," or something hokey like that. He'd seen too many families devastated by a child's illness, or a parent's inability to cope with hard news.

Why seek more risk than what life already provided in its cost of living?

"To each his own," he said. They'd just have to disagree.

"You have your stuff ready to go?"

He nodded and pointed to the small pack on the floor at his feet. She frowned and it felt as if he was being chastised by a schoolteacher. A hot schoolteacher he wouldn't mind being bent over a desk with, but still… He'd been out of education long enough, he forgot what it felt like to carry some impostor syndrome around. "Lila sent the email requesting you come prepared to do a short hike, right?"

"Yeah, but if you think we shouldn't because I didn't bring the right stuff—"

He absently put a hand on his own pack. He'd brought a lunch—takeout from the sub shop down the street from his Seattle condo—as well as a hat, sunblock, and a wool sweater, in case the sun dipped behind the range or clouds moved in. When he'd left the condo, he'd grabbed breakfast at the café with his neighbor, thinking his packing list was sufficient.

Now, though, it felt like a paltry offering to the mountain gods, considering everything Erin had packed. At a minimum, he looked as if he'd passed on the heavier pack to Erin. Not that he was against flipped gender roles, but it would be nice if he didn't seem like the weakest link on this venture.

"I've got it. I've done this a time or two." She sighed and grabbed a radio from its charger.

"You're bringing that, too?" he asked. She'd packed everything except the ambulance rig itself in her pack, it seemed. Was she just adding things to make him look bad?

She held up the walkie-talkie and made a show of adding it to the rig on her fleece.

"This?" He nodded.

She'd also put a bag in her rucksack that looked like it contained a surgical suite's worth of supplies. "Yeah. Out here, we don't stay far from ways of asking for help."

"Our cell phones won't work?" he asked. Her crooked smile, as if he'd said something juvenile or asinine, also said he was in over his head deeper than he'd thought.

"Nope. They won't work three feet outside this parking lot. But don't worry that pretty little head of yours. I've got everything we need in case of an emergency or inclement weather."

"I thought you said the weather was gonna be fine," he said. "What do you mean, 'inclement'?"

If he could have catalogued her looks so far, he'd have them in two categories: nonchalant and poised to kill. The one she shot him now was the latter.

"You're in the wilderness, or you will be. It doesn't care, nor think about human requests like sunny days and smooth paths. In fact, historically, that's not why people come to us. They want nature on full display and to be challenged."

He pinched the bridge of his nose. Yeah, he'd definitely bitten off more than he could chew with this woman. Was she serious with all this challenge-is-required-to-live-a-full-life stuff? Wasn't life hard enough without adding to it? There was no way she'd experienced the kind of loss he had, or she wouldn't be making statements like that.

Don't be a baby. Not everyone is out to get you, Reese. You two are just different, that's all.

He heard his conscience's advice in his sister's voice. Some days, it felt like all he had left of her besides the little girl at home that looked so much like the other women in his family, Allie included.

Never mind. It didn't matter if he and Erin were as different as night from day. Her proposal was a tough sell. Not just with him, but the board of Seattle Memorial Hospital. It would take an act of congress to get the board to sign off on a multimillion-dollar project in rural Washington when budgets were costing good programs in the city.

He should just make a show of checking her paperwork, decide it was too expensive, and put it in a filing cabinet somewhere. At least the board would be spared having to waste time with this coming across their desks.

Goodness knew his life would be easier, too. He could focus on getting his clinical study up and running, maybe even take up with that running club that ran the roads of Seattle. Anything but a special project that was so niche it might as well be a clinical research study. Why was it his turn to be in charge of proposals when he had to find a sitter and travel halfway across the state to assess the viability?

The man who'd retired and handed it off to Reese—Nick Remy—had done so with a warning: "If you don't at least go out there, she'll write you once a month and bug you until she gets a site visit. Learn from my mistake, son. Go early, so you can shut it down."

Reese didn't believe in deciding on such a huge project before he'd seen all there was on both sides of the argument—a site visit included—so he'd half heeded Nick's advice and set this up for his first month on the special-interests committee.

Who knew? Maybe it would be something worth pursuing.

"Let's take another look at your proposal before we leave so we can talk about the key points on the trail."

Nick was a little off base. The idea Erin had outlined was a good one from a needs-based perspective. And he'd do whatever it took to convince the board of that if—emphasis on *if*—she could prove the need for the clinic and its exorbitant costs. They didn't scare him like they had Nick.

The issue was, now that he was in Hoodsport, Reese realized Erin's proposal for the clinic wasn't anything he could believe in—not at first glance, anyway. It was an interesting idea—a fully functioning clinic that would take all the local and transient cases that were emergent enough to be transported, but where transport was impossible because of weather, or other circumstances. But he couldn't imagine much that would change his mind enough to go toe-to-toe with a financially strapped board to make the case on her behalf.

If anything, it was probably something a physician team should take on, not a whole hospital. He'd make that recommendation when he turned down the proposal as it was.

He was about to outline why it was an expensive proposition for an already strapped hospital system. But they were interrupted by the doors to the clinic flying open before he could follow through on that line of questioning.

"We've got a climber down," a man said. Blood covered the front of his shirt. "He's in my truck—can you help?"

"We've got him," Erin said. She grabbed a kit from a shelf and began running toward the exit.

Reese called after her, "Where do you need me?"

"I've got this," she said over her shoulder. He followed her out, anyway, and was met with her and the man, each holding up a young man who was battered on his whole right side.

"What happened?" Erin asked the man.

"I was hiking and saw him fall off a twenty-foot cliff. Landed on soft ground, but it was a helluva drop."

"Why does anyone do that without the proper safety equipment?" Reese asked. "Or at all. It's like he was asking for this." He couldn't wrap his head around the decision to purposely put oneself at risk. Not when there was plenty to love about life that was safe. Secure.

"We're looking at internal injuries, then," Erin said, ignoring him. "I'll do a workup and call for a flight to Seattle."

"I thought you said that wasn't a possibility."

Erin looked at him like she was shocked he was still there, still talking.

"It's not impossible. But in most of the weather we have around here it's inadvisable at best. Lucky for you—and the patient—you both came in on one of the best days we've had here."

She made a call on the radio to what sounded like a flight medic and then cut off the patient's shirt. He was bruised, and there were lacerations along most of the side of his body.

"They need to be cleaned while he's here to reduce the risk for infection," Reese said. Erin hooked up the leads to the patient's chest.

"I'm aware. I'm an EMT, remember?"

"I'll clean while you do the workup. I'm a doctor."

What was it with her assessment of him that always made him feel as if he was coming up short? And why did he care what she thought?

Because no matter how you feel about her, she's competent, and you'd like to be seen in that light by her.

She didn't answer, didn't even ask any follow-up questions, just handed him some disinfectant, a roll of gauze, and bandages. It was good enough.

They worked in silence, him cleaning, and her palpitating the abdomen and suturing the deeper wounds. The patient was unconscious but with regular breathing. He was steady, not in immediate external risk, but without state-of-the-art equipment—equipment an outpost wouldn't have—there was no way of knowing what was going on inside.

As if she'd read his mind, she said, "The clinic would have a fully functioning lab and imaging center."

"Is that kind of expense justified out here?" he asked.

"It's not unjustified when you compare the costs of transporting patients and caring for them off-site."

"Tell me more," he said. At this point, he was curious.

As he watched Erin make notes to hand off to the medics who would transport the patient to Seattle, and listened to her explain her rationale for the clinic, he was struck by her medical awareness, as well as her insight to what would be needed for a project like hers to get off the ground. He had to hand it to her. She was thorough.

More than competent, too. She was an expert, and far beyond what an EMT should be. Had she done any medical school? It didn't track that someone as invested in the medical world and her patients' interests would stop at an EMT license.

"You're really just an EMT?" he asked as she finished her last of a string of sutures along the patient's abdomen.

"Excuse me?" she asked. "EMTs are the backbone of medical practice and the front line of first responders. We save more lives per year than doctors."

He winced.

"That's not what I meant. It's just that you're good at this. I would have thought you were a nurse practitioner or a physician."

"Nope. Maybe at some point, when I was a kid allowed to dream, but I'm just an EMT. And proud of it."

He sighed and ran his hands through his hair. "You should be. I have incredible respect for first responders. It—it was meant as a compliment."

"Thanks, then. Alright, I'm gonna meet Hector outside and make sure it's a smooth transfer. We'll be ready to go after that. Grab a coffee or food if you want because there aren't stops on our hike. Just us and the nature you can't believe anyone enjoys."

She wheeled the patient out to the back as the sounds of an incoming helicopter took over the small space.

He didn't know what it was about this woman, but he just couldn't get it right with her. No matter what, he kept stepping in it. He'd be curious about her—why she was the way she was, why she'd stopped dreaming of being a doctor—if only finding out didn't mean he would need to spend more time talking to, and subsequently messing up with, the woman.

Damn. It was gonna be a long day, wasn't it?

CHAPTER THREE

It wasn't a hardship to work with Reese. In fact, surprisingly, they were a good team. He was quiet as he worked, no doubt afraid to speak up and have her bite his head off again. But he was a solid doctor and the calm was peaceful. He found his way around the single outpost room, with its rudimentary supplies they used to stock the ambulance, and only once commented under his breath how anyone who came in injured shouldn't have been out there in the first place.

If he wasn't such a risk-averse, indoor enthusiast, he'd be a good asset to the team she'd imagined when she'd outlined the nurse practitioners and physicians needed to keep a clinic running in a rural location.

But no. Reese Vallen was the last person she could imagine coming out here to visit, let alone relocate in Hoodsport. He didn't see the beauty Erin and the other mountaineers did.

Once Hector, her flight medic, came to pick up the climber and transport him, Erin cleaned up the makeshift treatment room. In reality, it was a storage space for the rig supplies, but a few years ago Erin had outfitted it with a table for patients that found their way to the outpost.

She'd even once used the stationary ambulance to perform basic surgery to extract a branch from a fallen hiker's leg. The weather had been too poor to drive the narrow roads and work on the patient at the same time, so she'd made a judgment call to not leave until the hiker was stable.

It'd paid off, and that was the day Erin had finished outlining her proposal for the clinic.

Since then, she'd pitched it more than a dozen times to anyone at Seattle Memorial who would listen, and this was the first time the person they sent to do a site visit actually followed through.

That had to be promising, right?

She glanced at Reese, who was tying laces to what appeared to be dry-weather hiking shoes. They hadn't been broken in at all and when he lifted one to tug the laces, she saw a sticker still on the clean soles. Good grief.

Was he really the one who was going to get it off the ground? She didn't think so, but what choice did she have except to throw everything at him she had and hope he saw what she did—people in Hoodsport and the surrounding area needed a top-notch medical facility.

They deserved one.

"You ready?" she asked.

Reese's grimace wasn't promising, but he nodded. "Ready as I'll ever be."

She sent one more text to her dad, knowing the cell service would be nonexistent in a minute or two.

Got delayed leaving the outpost. Heading out now, probably to the eastern ridge of The Brothers. Love you and see you tomorrow morning to take you to your appointment.

She sent a little prayer to whatever deity was in charge of the weather that the barometric pressure held steady then. Her dad's flare-ups when it dropped made travel to necessary medical appointments difficult, if not impossible.

It was a stern reminder of her personal reason for making sure this project happened.

When she was done, Erin mapped the trail she wanted to take as they left the outpost. She amended it from her original plan after noticing how ill-equipped Reese was.

Meanwhile, Reese was on his phone, "sending an email to the powers that be," a chore that ended as soon as they got not ten yards away from the outpost and lost service.

Told ya, she thought. Too bad she'd used up her allotment of snark with Reese and couldn't say that aloud.

"You weren't kidding," he grumbled, throwing his phone into a pack.

"Nope." She wasn't sure what else to add. Erin took the outdoors—and the consequences for disregarding it—seriously, and this guy clearly didn't. He might be good at medicine and patient care, at least from what she could see. But he didn't have a clue when it came to the kind of terrain her patients were traversing and what kinds of injuries could occur.

She steered them toward the eastern canyon, and even Erin had to admit the Olympic Mountains were showing off that afternoon. The sun-dappled cliffside was bathed in emerald green, a result of good water runoff this spring.

"So you don't do much hiking, huh?" she asked. He was fit enough, appearance-wise. Even his muscles had muscles on top of them. The difference between Reese's fitness and say, Hector's, was that the flight medic's muscles were earned in the terrain, forged by activity and the elements, while Reese's looked cultivated in a gym.

Not that she was complaining. If she had to take a suit from the city around, at least they'd had the good sense to send her someone who added to the view in front of her.

"Not really, no. I live in the city."

She let go a bark of a laugh. "Okay, sure. You live in a city surrounded by two of the most epic ranges in the Pacific Northwest, not to mention some of the best waterways this country has to offer."

He turned around to face her, and she had to admit, with his hair tousled by the breeze and some sun on his cheeks, this place looked good on him. That was the case with most people—they came alive in a different way out there. The trick was getting them there in the first place.

"Accidents in the Puget Sound area are one of the top three leading causes of death for Washington residents and visitors alike," he said. "Not exactly an advertisement for diving in."

Okay, so maybe Reese wasn't gonna build a summer home here, but she could give him that afternoon, a seed planted maybe.

"And Washington residents who don't die of cancer and heart disease, the other two leading causes I'm aware of, since I am a medical professional, too, have a relatively longer lifespan thanks to all the outdoor activities they take part in. Preventative medicine like getting natural vitamin D and moving your body outside are just as good for you as being in a gym. Better, even."

He turned back around and kept hiking up the slope. "That's not even counting the injuries sustained on this range. I just don't see the point. At least in my gym I can be sure I'll make it home alive."

"You're kidding, right?" She stopped walking. "Ignoring the fact that over a hundred male bodybuilders die each year, and countless others shorten their lifespan by taking supplements that are dangerous, are you telling me you don't take any risks?"

He turned back again and gave her a scowl. "Not if I can avoid them."

She looked down at his hand, where there was

a faint line indicating a ring had once sat on his left ring finger.

"You were obviously married, which carries its own risks, and I can tell you statistically that more people die as a result of awful partnerships than from enjoying beauty like this."

"My ex had the same idea you did. Which is why she left—" He paused and touched the space where the band used to be. "So, yeah, I know my opinions are unpopular. I'm used to being dismissed for them, but I have reasons for feeling the way I do."

Erin felt the heat not so much creep as flood her cheeks. *Dammit.* Why couldn't she keep from stepping in it with this man? He was infuriating, sure. And as different from her as a person could be, but hadn't she experienced the same loss? Her mother had left when she was in third grade because her dad couldn't quit the dangerous lifestyle she was pretty sure would kill him.

According to Erin's mom, she wasn't "going to sit around and watch you kill yourself and leave us behind." She'd tried to take Erin with her, but the only fate worse than death to Erin when she was a kid was leaving the streams and peaks behind their cabin. Leaving her dad.

It was hard not to have empathy for the man when she loved the same lifestyle he did; he'd never be happy in a city—hell, anywhere else for that matter. So how could *she* have been?

Well, she'd paid for that way of thinking in her own way, hadn't she?

She waited for him to add more, and when he didn't, she took a hesitant step forward and took his left hand in hers. Maybe it was inappropriate, but that was the thing about the great outdoors; it had a way of inspiring confidences and turning strangers into friends. She'd expected his hand to be smooth, the skin of a suit who sat behind a desk. But she was met with warm, rough hands and the juxtaposition confused her.

So did the heat building between their palms. She released his hand, but the lingering effects didn't abate.

"I'm sorry," she said. "It's none of my business, but I want you to know I've been left behind for my way of life, too." An understatement. *No one but my dad ever stuck around.* Not one friend from school, not one boyfriend, not her own mother.

"A spouse?" he asked. She shook her head.

"No one in that department wants to compete with the long hours and dangerous work. I've never been important enough to be promoted to spouse."

His crooked smile, higher on the left than the right, was adorable.

"I find that hard to believe." He shook his head as if realizing how close his statement came to being human and flirtatious. It'd been a bit since she'd engaged in witty banter with a handsome man—or a man in general, if she was honest with herself. "Anyway, none of that matters. The rising cost of health care in the city proves how ridiculous it would be to take on double that overhead with a rural satellite clinic."

She sighed, the cloud cover hitting her dew-spotted skin. It chilled her instantly. The only thing that didn't cool off immediately was her stomach and the place she'd touched Reese. That man might drive her insane as they worked through the problem of how to keep people safe on and off the mountain and in the Hood Canal, but he would be wholly tempting while he did it.

She rubbed her arms to transfer the heat from her palm to her exposed flesh.

"It's ridiculous not to. Think of the life-flight money you'll all save."

"Those are privately run."

Erin barked out another laugh. "Right. I forgot that those companies—even the ones running from the hospital itself—charge the customers directly. How silly of me. You really are looking at this through a myopic lens, aren't you?" Any kindness for the man was evaporating like the rain hitting the dry mountain faces off in the distance.

"I thought we had to hustle out of here so we avoided those clouds back there," he said, pointing to the gray-lined clouds on the horizon. She ignored him and the fact that they did indeed look closer…and more ominous.

"That's why you're here, you know," she said, grabbing a granola bar from her pack. "To help us find a way to mitigate the deaths and injuries these mountains dole out each year and, sure, consider the cost, but also to find a middle ground. Because, contrary to what you think, I don't want irresponsible risk, either. I want people to come out here, to see what fulfills them, and to make sure they are medically sound when they leave the park. And I can't do it alone. Will you at least try to be open-minded about why this is a necessity? Because telling people 'this is dangerous' isn't going to keep them out of the national park. So let's do what we can to support them. Okay?"

The look he gave her—his eyebrows pulled tight and his lips twisted in confusion—worried her. But then, the tension in his mouth released. It almost even resembled a smile at one point, and it was like the clouds now overhead had parted and allowed the sun back in.

Great. So her libido was involved now.

Careful, her heart whispered. *You're not allowed to crush on a man you're hoping will open up medical worlds for you and your dad. A man who thinks safety matters more than actually living. A man eerily similar to Ben.*

Ben, the first man to tell her she was crazy for staying in a small town, the first to leave her behind since her mom.

Erin knew that. But it didn't mean she couldn't appreciate the fine-looking addition to her hike while he was there with her. A drop of water landed on her forearm. Damn. They'd better hustle.

"I'll be open to the idea. I promise."

She nodded. That had to be enough.

He waved at the expanse of land. "For what it's worth, this place is pretty special. I'll give that to you."

She beamed. Okay, that was nice, too.

"I couldn't agree more. Now, yes, let's get back down before those ugly clouds decide to unleash on us."

No sooner were the words out of her mouth than the sky opened up on them, a torrent of cold water like a spigot from the sky. Reese started to jog down the trail.

"Careful," she warned, yelling over the sound of the water hitting the dry rocks and dirt at their feet. "It'll be slick. Better to go slow and take our time."

He nodded that he understood.

"Aghhh!"

She ran to Reese's side, but he was fine—the noise came from somewhere else. She gripped his biceps.

"Did you hear that?"

He stopped, but the rain made it hard to hear anything but it.

So much for keeping her dad safe tomorrow. He'd be in bed with oxygen by the time she got off the mountain today.

"Is anyone out there?" Erin yelled.

"I didn't hear a thing other than the storm. We gotta hurry, Erin. This doesn't look like it's gonna let up." Reese's eyes held a mild panic. This terrified him. She understood, but the hair standing on end on her arms had nothing to do with the temperature drop.

Her intuition said there was someone out there. If she was wrong, she would only cost them a few minutes of waiting. Yes, that could be the difference between life and death out here, but they were both medical professionals. They could afford it if it meant the possibility of saving someone else.

For a few seconds, there was nothing else.

“Help!” a distant voice called out. “I need help!” She heard the second part clearly, as if the person was next to them, but whoever it was had to be over the ridge at least.

“I heard it,” Reese said. His gaze focused where Erin’s was. “What do we do?”

“Dammit,” she said. “There’s a change of plan. I’m radioing for a chopper and going on a rescue.”

CHAPTER FOUR

THE CREASES IN his forehead deepened. He didn't like the idea any more than she appeared to, but what choice did they have?

Or rather, what choice did *he* have?

He wasn't on duty, wasn't employed by the backcountry ambulance service. But he was a doctor who'd promised to do no harm. Leaving someone in imminent peril because it made him deeply uncomfortable to be on the side of a mountain…well, it wasn't an option, no matter how much he wished it were.

"What do you need from me?" he asked.

"Do you remember the way back? No offense, but I don't need another liability out here."

He let that comment sink in. She'd given him the out he'd been hoping for.

And yet… His skin might be on fire imagining the danger they'd find themselves—or their patient—in, but he wasn't going to stand by and let her do this herself, either.

"I might not be the most adept out here, but I'm still an award-winning, double-board-certified pediatric surgeon. I'm not just a suit, Erin. And you and I worked well together. Let me help you."

She regarded him carefully, her eyes darting between him and where the cry for help had come from.

"Fine. But we've got to hurry. Try not to fall and make things worse."

He grumbled under his breath. That wasn't his plan, but he guessed he had her to thank for making him think about it. He watched each step on the way back toward the ridge, worried about what they'd find. He'd seen trauma, both man- and nature-inflicted, but he'd never practiced outside a sterile operating room.

The last thing he wanted was to become her worst nightmare out here—another risk she needed to mitigate because he didn't know what he was doing.

Erin was like a mountain goat, nimble and light on her feet. She radioed the outpost and got a hold of Lila, who sent in a call to Seattle for a helicopter; it would be faster than waiting for Hector to return from there after dropping off the hiker. They ran fast, and Reese was glad to see the time he'd logged on a treadmill, though not optimal for training on trails, had at least kept his cardio strength up to par.

The radio crackled and Reese's heart pounded in anticipation as much as with the strain of the impromptu race along a steep ridge.

Don't look down. Keep your eyes on the trail.

He couldn't hear what they said.

"Where will they meet us?" he asked.

She shook her head, sending a second spray of water his way.

"They aren't. Weather is too socked in where they're at."

"What are we supposed to do?" he asked. Anticipation sat on his skin as if the potential energy alone could fuel him.

"We check out the patient, then I radio down and ask Hector to fly up when he's back. His chopper's home base is at the outpost, which is closer, but it doesn't always pay to use it if Seattle will run."

"Won't the weather be an issue for us, too?"

"We can get around the storm cell and approach from the south with the wind in our favor, and our chopper is smaller, more agile."

Why did smaller seem like a bad thing?

They got to the edge of the cliff face and he let her peer over to survey what they were dealing with. Heights and him hadn't always been simpatico, not since he'd been on the search party for Allie and had slid down the embankment where her body was found. His dizziness had stayed with him while he vomited at the sight of her mangled, lifeless body.

He'd never recovered, not fully.

Would they find the same thing now? He shuddered to think so.

"Hey," Erin called out over the cliffside.

Please don't get closer, he thought. Vertigo set in.

"We're here to help. How many are down there?"

There was a beat of silence, then a weak voice said, "Just me."

Erin grabbed a coil of rope from the pack and tied an end to a spruce tree, then the other to her waist in what looked like a crude attempt at a harness.

"What are you doing?" he asked. This was like something out of an adventure movie—not real life, where the consequences were final and damning. Water poured off Reese's face like he was standing under a waterfall. Speaking of those… He wiped his eyes and squinted. Rivulets had already formed along the opposite side of the valley, so it looked as if they were in a rainforest.

Which, he supposed, they were.

Erin walked to the edge of the cliff and tugged on the tension of her rope. After loosening it, she leaned over backward and stepped down the cliff face.

His stomach was in knots. What the hell?

Shit. Doing this at all was dangerous and doing it in this weather was asinine.

"You're good at what I've seen you do so far, but this is insane. Jumping off a cliff face isn't the move, Erin."

She met his gaze; her hair and clothing were as soaked as his. The only difference was, it looked as if the material of her outfit was better suited to the environment based on how it hung on her. His cotton T-shirt clung to his frame and only once did her gaze dip to the tight fabric against his skin.

"You want to go over? I'm happy to give up this part of the gig, but either way, one of us is rescuing the patient and bringing them to safety."

He sighed. He genuinely didn't know which was worse—watching her careen off a cliff face, or doing it himself.

"Wait, where are you bringing them? You can't climb back up a cliff face with an injured person."

She spun around in her rope contraption and his stomach flipped.

"See that field over there? There's a trail if we keep going the way we were running. It'll take too long for me to do, but I'll rig a stretcher with my tarp and poles, drag whoever I need to, and meet you. We need to be visible and in a place Hector can land."

"I can help. Let me come down with you."

"No. I need you to get something together for a sterile field. Set it up in the field and leave room for Hector to land. He'll be here soon, and we'll need to make a quick exit so we aren't stuck in the valley until the storm lets up."

"Then let me come. Please. I'll run to the field once I know you're safe and don't need my help with the patient. Besides, you have the equipment I'll need to build a sterile field, anyway." He had a raincoat he could rig up to block the rain, but her pack was infinitely better for all the contingencies she'd anticipated. "I'll make it to where the patient is and then flag Hector. Deal?" Damn, he wished he'd done even a little bit of research. Not for the first time, Reese was impressed with how prepared Erin was, how competent and steady she seemed.

Who takes care of her while she's taking care of everyone else?

He'd wondered that about her before. But now, he had a whole different set of questions, all of them inappropriate.

Is she seeing anyone? his brain asked, anyway.

What did that matter? Not just because they were standing on a literal precipice in the rain about to perform some death-defying stuff to save a patient, but because…well, he was who he was.

Who's that? his subconscious asked as if that particular part of his brain hadn't been running the show for the past few years.

He tried to parse that out as she nodded and let out enough slack that he had rope to make his own harness and let himself down.

Well, hell. Apparently, he was a man who jumped off cliffs for a woman he found intriguing.

Not that she was the reason, that he wouldn't have done this for the patient if she wasn't here, but the two were literally connected by a rope at this point, so it was impossible to distinguish between what was Erin's pull over him and what his driven sense of care was responsible for. All he knew was that he felt more alive—more himself—than he had in years.

Speaking of the rope she'd handed him, what was he supposed to do with it? He tried to follow her instructions and came up with…*something*. Whether it would hold or not remained to be seen.

"It looks good," she called. He exhaled and followed her over the edge. It was terrifying, but also…freeing. The water made the rope slick, but he glanced down and she was moving hand over hand. He copied her movements and allowed the adrenaline—usually a trigger for him to flee, defend himself, or freeze—to course through him. As much as he hated to admit it, it was a cool experience, akin to saving a life in the ER.

Before he could think about it, his feet were on the ground and something about him was different. Not fundamentally, but a part of his heart had been unlocked.

Whoever he'd been moments ago was still present, and… He was also a man who'd rapelled down a cliff face.

"Good, isn't it?" she asked. He realized that despite their circumstances, he was smiling. He pulled her into a side hug, the feel of her both calming and exhilarating in its own way.

"Sure is."

"Okay, let's get to work."

They undid their harnesses and jogged toward where she'd heard the cry for help, and sure enough, there was a climber, with rope not unlike the piece they'd used still tied around a legitimate harness. It was frayed at one end, painting a picture of what had happened.

She was curled around a leg that appeared to be

broken, though thankfully, there wasn't any broken skin. They could splint this and make it safe for the woman to travel, at least at first glance. Like the man who'd been brought in earlier to the outpost, there was the risk of internal bleeding.

At least she was still conscious, and not fully succumbing to shock, since that was a real possibility out here.

Reese got to work setting up a sterile field with a tarp from the backpack and some poles to make a shelter first. Erin talked to the patient and found out she'd fallen two hours earlier. Not a dangerous amount of time, but they needed to care for her injuries as soon as possible. Erin also discovered that she was with a partner and didn't know where they'd gone.

"You're the second climber we've seen today," Reese said. They both shot him a look while Erin splinted the injury—Erin with curiosity, and the patient with fear.

"There's not a high statistic they were together," Erin cautioned him. He understood, but one thing he did know from his time practicing pediatrics was that sometimes the obvious answer—not just the simplest—was the right one. Often, it was also the hardest one to articulate with a patient.

Obvious abuse shoved behind excuses like "fell off a bike."

A pregnancy missed because of implantation bleeding despite a thousand other symptoms in favor of the obvious.

A cancer diagnosis the patient "knew" but didn't want to admit to themselves.

He didn't believe in coincidences, or easy ways out of tough situations—life was beautiful in its complexity, and it took work to keep it that way. And to keep everyone safe.

"Did your partner have a tattoo of a dog on his right arm? I think it was a basset hound?"

The woman's face contorted in what began as a smile, then morphed into a sob when she realized what that meant.

"Yes," she wailed. "It's a tribute to Gary, our little guy. He died two years ago and Andy—my husband—got the tattoo to remember him. I had hoped he'd just get the paw prints, but no, he needed the whole slobbering beast. I gave him so much hell for it." The woman choked out a breath, then wheezed in a new one. She was close to hyperventilating. "I was always giving him hell about something. Even today, when he went off to scout a new route because I was taking too long with this one, and I wanted to leave because of the weather, he told me I was being silly, that nothing was going to happen to us—"

She choked on her words and any air she tried to take in. Panic was on the horizon if not already using its icy grip to smother the poor woman.

"Nothing happened to him that can't be fixed," Erin said. Now, it was Reese's turn to shoot her a look of concern.

"That isn't true," he whispered. "We didn't have

the equipment to do a thorough scan and rule out anything serious."

"Exactly," she growled back. "It would be great if we had that equipment, but we don't, so I have to rely on what we have available to us."

He pinched the bridge of his nose. They were wasting time talking about the proposal when they needed to meet the helicopter.

"We can revisit the reason I'm here once she's safe." To the patient, he added, "We'll make sure the flight medics pass on that your husband was their transport earlier and that you'd like information about how he's doing."

She nodded but was having trouble taking in a full breath. Whether it was from the pain, or news that her husband was injured, or both, it didn't matter. She was near a panic attack that would make transporting her difficult if not impossible.

"Do you have any benzodiazepines or SSRIs in that bag?" he asked. "She's close to a panic attack. We need to calm her down, or that, combined with her fracture, could cause a stroke."

Erin nodded, at least in agreement about that.

"Hey, Hanna?" she asked. Reese had missed the woman's name until then. Erin had exceptional bedside manner, especially considering she never really worked with a "bedside" to speak of. "We're gonna need to give you a relaxant so you don't hyperventilate and hurt yourself more, okay?"

Hanna didn't answer. Even from a distance, Reese could hear that her breaths were shallow.

He'd moved to the edge of the tree line to keep an ear out for the helicopter, but didn't want to leave Erin's sight in case she needed help.

"Hanna, we need to give you this—is there anything we need to know before we inject the meds?"

Reese saw that she had a painkiller on deck, too. That wasn't a bad idea. He'd just make a note to let the medic know. The chain of custody with patients was so vital in patient care. It was challenging in a normal hospital environment—out here, it was imperative and tricky as hell.

Again, he had a sense of awe watching Erin track everything, care for their patient, and talk to her as if she'd done this a hundred times.

She probably had.

"I'm pregnant," the woman said. Reese hissed in a breath, earning another look of warning from Erin.

He heard the helicopter in the distance, which was the only reason why he didn't address the concern sitting on his tongue. Why people did this for fun was beyond comprehension. It was harrowing, dangerous, and potentially fatal. Sure, he'd felt good learning something new on this rescue, but still…

To be pregnant meant putting not only herself, but also her child at risk. He couldn't comprehend it.

"You should stay with her while I go make sure Hector can see us," he said. There was no way he was spending another minute out here if he didn't have to.

She nodded, her expression sharp.

"Thank you, Reese, for your help and being out here. I'm sorry I brought up the clinic, but can't you see why it's necessary? There are families we'd save."

He liked this woman—her dedication to her patients and brilliance in the field were enough to draw his attention. Never mind how knockdown beautiful she was.

One thing he couldn't quite put a finger on was why she was so okay with the inherent danger others put themselves in, especially when tourists did it unprepared and for "fun," putting her at risk in her job.

The whir of the helicopter blades got louder, and thankfully, the rain had let up just enough that he had a place to land.

"Erin," he called. "Time to go!" He flagged Hector, whose small craft landed safely, and then ran to help Erin carry Hanna to the transport.

They loaded her and strapped her in, and Hector took off immediately. This was the second risky, new thing Reese had done today and he wasn't sure he wanted to make a habit out of it.

Once they were out of the canyon and heading through the pass, Reese took a moment to observe where they were. There was nothing out there. Just the Pacific Ocean behind them, and pure forest, lakes, and peaks between them and the east, where good medical care was.

Only when they'd touched down in Seattle did he exhale. Hanna was delivered to her team of providers and they promised her a reunion with her husband, who largely seemed out of the woods, though the team said he probably shouldn't go climbing for at least six months.

Or ever again, Reese thought.

Hector asked them if they wanted to stay and wait out the rain, or go back.

"The storm looks like we've passed through the worst of it," Erin said, checking an app on her phone.

Reese didn't care. He had no desire to get back in that bird. He was home and should just stay in Seattle, let Erin know he'd "think about" her proposal and get back to her.

Her phone rang in her hand and she frowned.

"What's up, Lila?" She put the phone on speaker.

"You close? We've got a group of hikers who came in dehydrated and with minor frostbite. I need you and that bird back quick. Some of 'em are gonna need transport. If that doc from earlier wants to come, we could use his help, too."

Hector nodded and started the preflight checklist again.

Reese glanced at her, could see the question in her eyes. Sending her alone through the pass seemed like a cowardly exit when they'd been such a good team twice now… Besides, his keys and wallet were back in Hoodsport. The sooner he retrieved them, the sooner he could head back to his daughter. At least she was at his mom's tonight, so he didn't have to rush.

A whole night in rural Washington with Erin sent shivers up his spine for some reason. Maybe it was just the change in barometric pressure.

"I'll go back with you," he said. He caught the hint of a smile tugging at the corners of her mouth, but she simply nodded.

"Okay. Thanks."

"The weather looks good?" Reese asked.

Erin showed him. Sure enough, the cell had dissipated, but he knew enough not to trust the weather up there to stay for long.

"We should go now, though, just in case," Erin insisted. He was glad they were in agreement.

"You got it, boss," Hector said. In a matter of minutes, they were in the air again, and Reese's stomach was back to residing in his chest cavity. When they hit a bump, Erin grabbed his hand, and he was thankful for it. Somehow, her proximity calmed him in a way that no one else could.

Scientists would have a field day studying that notion—especially given the very different lifestyles they led. Speaking of…

"Why don't you care about all these people putting themselves at risk?" he asked. She hadn't let go of his hand and he couldn't say he minded. "I mean, considering what you do for a career… isn't it all too much? Don't you ever just want to scream at them that they're in danger and should knock it off?"

She gazed out the open helicopter door, her eyes fixed on the horizon, which went up and down with the rugged peaks and valleys. If he was in the mood, he was pretty sure there was a metaphor in there, somewhere.

"If I did, I'd be a hypocrite. I mean, I hike out here, make my peace with the danger and risk, and let it keep me humble. If I didn't do my part to help educate, to mitigate and repair risk gone wrong, I'd lose a part of what makes me who I am. I like helping people who only want to push the boundaries of their own limits."

Then there was a sudden dip in the chopper.

"Sorry," Hector said through gritted teeth. "Weather's rough up here—looks like it isn't as clear as the weatherman predicted. Gonna take a side route."

Reese hissed an inhale as the chopper veered. He didn't like the sound of "rough" weather, going off course, or the concern in Hector's voice. He didn't know the man at all, but figured it didn't bode well for a helicopter pilot to be so worried about conditions he likely flew in regularly.

The helicopter wove and dipped again, and this time, Hector did more than grimace. He cursed and yelled as he fought the controls.

A sudden burst of light in front of them sent the machine—and its passengers—careening down.

All three of them screamed, and Reese grabbed tight to Erin, who was seated by the open door.

"Get over here," he screamed over the now-deafening roar of the combination of the blades and the pelting rain, and pointed to the other side of his seat. She nodded, fear in her eyes. He never let go of her hand as she unstrapped and moved over him.

No sooner had she edged next to him than an alarm beeped overhead and Hector could barely be heard as he shouted something at them.

Reese wasn't sure what it was, until Erin repeated it.

"Brace for impact," she yelled, barely strapping herself in before the chopper lurched and fell out of the sky.

CHAPTER FIVE

ERIN'S CHEST HEAVED. She gasped, but…couldn't draw a breath. Finally, it came, rough and gravelly, and it burned. She struggled to open her eyes. Something sat on her chest, something heavy.

The smell of burned metal and flesh singed her nostrils, and she gagged. The metallic taste of blood on her tongue made the nausea worse. As her body woke up from whatever nightmare it was in, what she saw was worse.

Smoke filled the small, confined space she was in, which was mangled with wires and buttons, including a crackling, unusable radio. And a man was draped over a part of what looked like a rucksack, which was sliced open and spilling its contents like guts.

Reese.

It took her a minute, and then it all hit her as if she was reliving the past half hour again.

The fallen hiker. Climbing down to rescue her.

Reese's help, even though he must have been so scared.

Hector's chopper rescuing all of them and taking them to Seattle Memorial.

The flight home.

The weather…

The crash.

The sounds and smells and fear all came back in a flood, and she tried to move to the unconscious man—*Reese! Please be okay*—but straps held her down. Urgency attacked her system.

She'd been so indifferent to the man, but the idea of losing him—not The Suit attached to making her dream of a clinic a possibility, but the guy who'd shown up in his most vulnerable state and done what was needed to support her… It was untenable.

"Please," she whispered, pushing the release button on the seat belt. Nothing happened. The softness turned to a shout. *"Reese!"*

She strained for the supplies bleeding out of the rucksack and her fingertips touched a plastic bag. She moved it and a glimmer of metal caught the waning light from a cracked window to her left.

A scalpel. She needed to get it closer. It was just out of reach, so she tried to reach. She could feel the pressure of the belt across her sore chest, but it didn't deter her. She needed to free herself so she could care for Reese, and who knew the state Hector was in.

Panic nipped at her but she ignored it.

Finally, the tips of her fingers made contact and she was able to angle the scalpel kit toward her.

She snatched it up, and in seconds was freed and at Reese's side.

Her entire body was sore, but didn't feel like anything was dire. All that mattered was making sure Reese was okay.

He had steady breathing sounds, as well as no visible contusions. Likely, he was just knocked out. She dug in the sack he was prostrate on and found smelling salts. In seconds, Reese's eyes shot open.

"What the...?" he asked. She put a hand on his cheek. His eyes were wild with concern and confusion—much as hers had been until a few minutes ago—but when they reached hers, his pupils narrowed and his breathing regulated.

"We were in a crash," she told him. She kept one hand on his cheek, and used the other to unbuckle him. He sat up and she was relieved that he was able to do so with such ease. From the looks of the mangled helicopter, the crash had been horrific. "How do you feel?"

"Like my helicopter fell out of the sky," he joked. A giggle escaped her chest, and it was followed by more laughter until she was doing some ugly blend of laughing and crying. He smiled and it was all she needed. "How are you?" he asked.

He used his thumbs to dry her tears and cup her cheeks. She tried to resist the urge to lean into him but it was futile. His presence was the only thing tethering her to calm.

"I'm okay. I'm bruised, and I feel like I'll find

some cuts, but I don't think anything is broken or bleeding."

"I'm so glad. I can't believe that happened. What did Hector say caused the crash?"

Her eyes filled with panic again. She could feel it spreading from her core out to the tips of her fingers and toes, which tingled.

"Hector," she whispered. "I don't know where he is, or how he is doing. My immediate concern was you. We need to—"

He nodded and glanced at the space between the seats to the cockpit. It was empty. Reese moved toward where the door would have been if a giant tree wasn't in their way.

It looked like the only way out was through the shattered front window of the chopper. That meant avoiding glass and debris that was everywhere after the harsh landing.

"I can go look if you need to take a second here," he told her. She shook her head.

"No, I've got this. I'm fine. Besides, you're forgetting, this is my territory. Literally and figuratively."

He'd been so brave. And here he was, showing up for her instead of being another…what had she called him? A liability?

She should have been more open-minded, like she'd asked him to be. Oh, well. She'd be better going forward.

Her heart warmed when he put his hands on her hips and helped her from the wreckage.

You don't have to be that *much better*, her sassy conscience chimed in. Not that it was wrong, but Erin did wonder when the last time she'd let herself just…lust after someone. Not since she could remember. It was always work, work, care for dad, more work.

Well, now's not the ideal time to start crushing on a guy. Maybe first survive this ordeal.

Point made.

She focused on the landscape when she got out of the rig, her eyes scanning for something that didn't belong. Reese must have noticed it at the same time Erin did because they both lunged toward the dark black heap of fabric at the base of a tall spruce.

They reached his side at the same time.

"He was thrown from the front," Erin said. The bruising and coagulated blood said they'd all been unconscious for probably ten minutes, and Hector was the worst of them all by a long shot. The back of the helicopter had fared significantly better than the front—the only thing that saved them, most likely. Hector's arm was clearly broken in at least one place and his breathing was thready as Erin leaned in and listened close. "Probably a pneumothorax."

"Can we get help out here? He'll need a transport."

Erin shut her eyes tight, willing all the strength she'd cultivated to come to her.

"He won't make a transport even if we could

radio one, or even if they could land here, or even if we knew where 'here' was."

Reese was nodding along, likely realizing, as she was, how dire things were.

"Tell me what you need from me. I've done a trach, but my hand is numb."

"Oh, no. Are you worried—"

"No," Reese said. "It's probably just a pinched nerve. But I'll talk you through the procedure."

"I've done one before. It wasn't pretty, but I know what I'm doing."

Reese's eyes widened. "You did a trach in the field?"

"Yep. But he sounds like he'll need a chest tube. I've done one of those, too."

He seemed to be mulling it over, weighing the risk versus reward. She understood. A surgery like that wasn't advised to be done by an EMT in the field unless it was medically mandated. And out here? With no way to get their patient to a more sanitized, safe environment? Yeah, "not advisable" was an understatement.

Then there was the matter of her certification. Technically, Reese should be the one to perform the lifesaving procedure based on his medical degree alone. But his hand would complicate things and they needed to get this right—they only had one shot to save Hector's life. She could do it.

"Do it," he said. He grabbed her hand and squeezed. Her arm was sore, the adrenaline from the crash wearing off. Her whole body felt…awful.

But she couldn't concern herself with that. Not yet. "And use me as a second, okay? Just tell me what you need."

"Thank you. For the trust, and support. I'll need both." She gave him a list of things to find in the packs, and what to bring if those couldn't be easily accessed or found after the crash. Time was their enemy.

Luckily, Reese was back in less time than it took her to set up their second sterile field—or as close to it as they could make it. He'd found most of what she wanted and all of what she needed, including her water pouch. She sliced off Hector's shirt and vest, and, yes, found significant bruising on his chest, indicating a pneumothorax, as she'd expected.

She hesitated over his elk tattoo. She'd been there when he'd gotten it after his dad died, had held his hand and witnessed his tears as he got the tribute inked on his body forever.

In cutting into him, there was no way to avoid slicing at least part of the antlers, and she just hoped he'd be okay with it.

If he lives, he'll be fine. He'll be grateful you saved him. But her worry was like gravity, keeping her down. Until Reese took her hand, placed a scalpel back in it.

"You have this," he told her. "Visualize what you need to do, not anything else."

She exhaled. Her nerves were on edge, her worry

a hot liquid thing that replaced the blood in her veins. If she messed up…

He placed her hand with the instrument on Hector's chest.

"He's like any other hiker up here. Just picture the wound that needs healing," Reese said. That was such sound, simple advice. If only she could apply it to her life outside medicine…

She couldn't think of Hector as anything other than a patient. Imagining his young wife, six months pregnant and waiting on him at home, was a recipe for disaster. He was her patient and she was his medic. Period.

"Thank you. Okay, let's do this." She gave Hector a dose of the morphine from the traveling med kit on the chopper, and as a backup, placed a stick between his teeth in case the pain woke him up from his shock-induced coma. She made a six-inch lateral incision down Hector's chest while Reese staunched the bleeding. Hector didn't wake up. He wasn't doing well. This would be touch and go. "It's his right lung, like we thought. I'm going to make an incision and it's going to relieve the pressure," she told Reese. He smiled up at her and she was struck again at how beautiful that smile was. How beautiful the man was. "He might wake up when we do that. Be prepared to hold him down."

He nodded, his presence so very grounding.

"Got it. Keep talking me through it, Erin. I'm here."

She cringed. "Oh, right. I keep forgetting you know what you're doing. You're an actual doctor."

He shook his head. "Don't. You're far more experienced in emergency medicine than me. My specialty isn't useless out here, but it's also not going to really do much with my hand like this. You're the best chance this guy has, so talk me through it."

She bit her lip and kept going, talking as she cut. Reese followed the instructions she gave while she talked, using rubbing alcohol to clean, cut, and sanitize her hydration pack hose. He gave her a look that seemd to say "are you sure?"

She shrugged. There weren't a lot of options in the Washington wilderness. It wasn't as if a surgical tray, overhead lights, and a chest tube were going to magically appear.

As she placed a tube in the pleural space, a hiss of air escaped, and the man's eyes shot open, like Reese's had. They darted around, unsure of what was happening. Unlike Reese, however, the pain set in and Hector screamed. The instability of her patient was going to make this ten times more difficult.

"Give him another round of morphine," Reese instructed. Now, it was her turn to question Reese's tactics. Her eyebrows raised in concern while Hector's cries echoed off the nearby canyon walls. They also dug inside her heart and clawed at it.

"Won't it be too much?" She'd just given him a dose minutes ago and they didn't have a monitor to check his vitals. Everything they were doing was by feel, sight, and instinct.

"His body is burning it off. Trust me, he needs this if we're gonna continue."

"Okay. I trust you." Not because she didn't have a choice, but because he'd earned that in small ways over several hours, and hadn't been wrong yet.

She gave Hector another dose, and sure enough, he calmed sufficiently that she could close most of the wound and disinfect the area. She bandaged him up as best she could while Reese built a shelter out of some canvas he'd found in the downed chopper. It was designed with grommets for emergency tenting, and would have to do for now, until she could look for something more permanent.

Reese's effort was rudimentary at best, and a clear indicator the man hadn't done much camping, either. She finished cleaning up and they moved the half-sleeping Hector to the shelter, where Erin set up a med station. They'd be there until they were rescued, so they'd better make sure they could keep Hector alive while they were stranded.

On that end, Reese had gone in search of Hector's satellite phone now that the helicopter radio was trashed and Erin's wouldn't reach a base this far out. She finished in the tent and built a fire.

"It's not that cold anymore. Should we conserve wood?" he called from the wreckage as smoke billowed above them.

"This isn't only for heat tonight. Right now, it's

our only form of communication with the outside world," she replied. "It's our chance at rescue."

He stopped digging in a bag and met her gaze. "Damn," he said.

"Yep."

They worked in silence, the whimpering coming from the shelter a morbid soundtrack to their situation. Hector was suffering and needed medical help. Erin met Reese at the wreck and started making piles of supplies. Food was at a premium, with a few MREs and some cans of soup that looked like they'd been around when Erin was born. There were some protein bars buried in the bottom of a sack Hector had brought that might hold them over longer.

Water was scarce—only two one-gallon jugs hadn't spilled. Luckily, Erin could hear a creek nearby, so that might be a saving grace if it was moving enough to keep the summer algae off the surface of the water.

Medicine was actually what they seemed to have most of. She found a tray of morphine and syringes, some other over-the-counter pain meds they could crush and put in Hector's water, and a range of bandages and disinfectants. The coup de grâce was a box-store-size bottle of antibiotics. That would be vital to prevent infection in Hector's open wound.

For being in one of the most precarouss situation imaginable, they weren't in the worst shape.

"Yes!" Reese shouted. He stormed over to her, a satellite phone raised high in the air. About two steps from her, he tripped on a rock in the makeshift campsite and almost went down. She met him, arms outstretched, intent on catching the phone if it fell. They needed it.

Luckily, he steadied himself and her open arms actually met…him. He closed the last step on purpose, handing her the phone with a sheepish grin.

"Almost screwed that up, too," he said.

"What do you mean, 'too'?" she asked. "You've been great up here."

"I dunno. I've definitely felt more like that liability you warned me about."

"I'm sorry if I—"

"No. You were right. Maybe I wouldn't have been a liability at one point in my life, but I've been so wrapped up in—in my own stuff I forgot how to play to my strengths. That seems to be changing lately, though."

She wrapped her arms around his middle and gazed up at him. He did seem different.

"Is this okay?" He nodded and took her in a tight embrace, wincing as her hands trailed across his chest. "Sore?"

He nodded. "I think I've got some cuts I'll have to attend to at some point." She moved back, but he pulled her tight. "Don't go. I needed a hug. That was—"

"Scary as hell?" she offered. He chuckled. She wanted to ask him more about what had been making him unsure of himself, but now wasn't the time. Not in his arms.

"That might be the understatement of the century, but yeah. My heart rate might never calm down."

Erin knew what he meant, but partially because the man in her arms raised hers in a way she hadn't anticipated… He both calmed and unnerved her. It was more disorienting than trying to figure out where they were in the Olympic Range.

"Wanna try this?" he asked. She nodded. Thank goodness Hector had a satellite phone onboard. She'd be adding one to her pack if—when—they made it off the mountain.

The sat phone crackled to life and Erin almost sobbed with relief.

"Libby," Reese whispered. He wiped at his eyes. "Sorry. Just worried about my family. She's my daughter."

"Start with her," she said. How terrifying. He had a daughter and was stuck on a mountain?

"Thank you." He stepped back and dialed a number. "Hey, Mom. It's me." There was a pause. "Yeah. I'm not gonna be home right away. I'm needed here, so is there a way you can—"

Another pause, longer this time.

"Thanks. I'll call you later and keep you updated. Love you. Tell…" His voice lowered. "Tell Libby hi and that I love her, too, please." He hung up, his voice scratchy.

"Why didn't you tell her?" she asked.

"I didn't want to worry her. She's so sensitive

after certain things in our past." Another thing she'd log away to ask later if she got the chance.

"Okay. I understand. I'll reach out to Lila and let her know we won't be back to help. She'll call in some of the younger EMTs."

The phone beeped, and she groaned.

"Low battery."

"Shit. If I'd have known, I would have—"

She shook her head. "It's fine. I'll see if the chopper's battery can charge it." If not, they were superscrewed, since no one, not even Reese's mom, knew where they were.

"Um, we should make a schedule to keep an eye on him. Each take four-hour sleep and food shifts while the other person takes care of Hector."

She nodded. "That's a good idea. I'll take the first one if you're okay with that."

He tightened his grip on her waist and nodded against her head. She must smell like hell. She considered going to wash in the creek, but what would she change into? Besides, that was such a first-world problem to consider when a man was struggling to stay alive in the shelter next door.

"Erin, I—" Reese leaned his head on hers. "I'm glad you're here. I know why you do what you do, and I may never agree with people who put themselves at risk for recreation, but what you do to keep them safe is incredible. You were incredible." Erin's skin warmed with the compliment. "I'll find a way to charge the phone so you're not stuck with me."

She leaned over and planted her lips on Reese's.

"I'm not stuck with you. Not like that," she whispered. He searched her eyes and kissed her back.

She wouldn't be able to come up with a reason why she'd kissed him, except that she had to. Since he'd come into her life, she'd been magnetically drawn to him in a way she couldn't explain. She'd done it—kissed him—without expecting anything other than satisfying a deep curiosity. Maybe she was also hoping for a small distraction from the pervasive sense of doom that had fallen over them when they'd discovered Hector with such a serious injury. From forgetting about the last man she'd kissed, and who'd left her for something she couldn't provide—security. Safety. A benign city life.

Something like where the man kissing her lived.

What she hadn't counted on was how the feel—and taste—of him would undo her. Heat blossomed in her belly and erased any aches her body had endured. In fact, it made her feel…good.

Even excusing the crash, she couldn't recall the last time she'd felt content, let alone happy. And here she was, in the middle of nowhere, facing particularly dire circumstances, and she was both of those things.

She opened her mouth to deepen the kiss and was brought deeper into the moment. His moan of pleasure brought her back to reality, and she broke the kiss. She bit her lip and gazed up at him.

"That was—"

"It was," she answered.

She kissed him again, this time just a peck.

"I've got to go," she whispered against his lips. He nodded. "It's my shift." He nodded again, though neither of them moved.

Finally, rustling and a groan from the makeshift shelter was enough to break whatever spell they were under, and she stepped back.

"I'll make us a shelter for tonight. I saw another, smaller canvas and a couple of bags," he said.

Erin headed to the shelter and wondered what it all meant. The crash, Hector's injury…her growing feelings for the man she was trapped in the wilderness with. She'd have gone beyond kissing if she'd stayed there, she was sure of it.

What did that say about her? About her working relationship with Reese?

What does it matter? You're lost and injured in the woods, and no one has come to find you. Let yourself off the hook.

She was never really good at that, though, was she?

The question she couldn't escape, especially not with the taste of him still on her lips, was whether those feelings were a result of the trauma they'd experienced, or if there was something real to them.

Either way, the danger facing her suddenly felt very real.

CHAPTER SIX

REESE ROLLED OVER onto his back, the sleep sack restricting his movements. He wasn't upset about it, though. How could he be, when it was the only thing protecting him from the elements? Well, it and Erin.

He warmed when he thought of how strong she'd been, and also at the strength she'd drawn out in him. In the office, she'd been sassy and clipped, but when things took a turn for the worse out in the field, she'd trusted his expertise, limited as it was, and had shown nothing short of grace and patience. If he was being honest, they were a good team.

Erin was calm and measured, where Reese was driven and meticulous. To be honest, he was still in shock at so much from that afternoon—that they were there at all being an all-encompassing one—but there were three things that plagued him and drove away sleep.

First, that Erin was an EMT, not a general surgeon or something...bigger. She certainly used her talents in her occupation, but her potential was stagnant and almost wasted.

Second, and related to the first, was that Erin had been right. The weather was too wild to attempt the flight back. She'd been called back, but he could have said no. That the weather could shift.

But how could I have known? I didn't grow up here...

Sure, a patient had made it to safety, barely, but they had a new patient, and they had only barely avoided having three casualties. This meant a lot, not only in examining his own decision-making that day, but also in seeing her side of why the clinic would be not just welcome, but necessary.

He'd be changing his recommendation to the board, that was for certain. They needed to find a way to provide services to Hoodsport and the surrounding communities. He wasn't sure they'd buy it, but he had to try, right?

The third revelation was the worst, the one that affected him deeper than the rest, and what was keeping him up right now.

He'd felt something between him and Erin when they'd been alone in the helicopter on the way back. Hell, if he was being honest, he'd experienced an attraction to her the minute he'd seen her, but it was disguised as disdain since she'd been less than perfect at that moment. What that rash judgment said was more about him, than her. She'd been nothing but professional from that moment on.

It was the transition to other feelings beyond attraction that was interesting.

He'd noticed a calm when she was around, something that he'd only felt before Allie's death, and after, around his daughter—like Erin was home, a safe space. It was even more interesting that this occurred in the middle of the most unsafe environment he'd ever physically been.

His phone was long past dead, or he'd open up his notes app and try to write his way through processing this new-to-him information.

Either way, he was supposed to be asleep, but it was hard to not stay vigilant when Erin was working with their patient. They'd agreed that the more efficient use of their time was to take shifts caring for Hector, now that he was stable, but that hadn't worked for Reese. He wanted to help, wanted to talk to Erin, wanted not to be alone with his thoughts.

The moans of discomfort from the shelter next door had abated, meaning that hopefully, Hector was getting rest. Thank goodness, too, since the man had been through it. His pneumothorax needed more medical attention than just the tube from Erin's water pouch, but at least, if Erin hadn't come running out, he could trust that Hector was good at the moment.

He heard the whoosh of fabric of the semisterile field they'd made out of the spare tent and his stomach tightened. For some reason, no matter what they'd just been through, he was nervous to spend a night alone in a makeshift tent with Erin. Not that he thought she'd do anything, but because when she'd offered a hug, he'd taken it. A kiss? The same thing. What would he want if she was close enough that he could touch…more of her?

Then there was the rest of what she brought out in him. Her proximity to him undid his tightly constructed rules about how life should be.

He'd followed those over the advice of people who knew better, and look where they'd ended up.

As Erin entered their sheltered space, he wondered what life would look like if he let her keep undoing his worries. He couldn't allow that mindset to take him too far away from the values he'd lived by, but it wasn't all bad imagining following through on his attraction to her. He had no idea how she felt about him, aside from labeling him "The Suit" before they'd met.

Gosh, that seemed like years ago with all they'd been through since.

"How's Hector?" he asked.

"You're awake," she noted. Her voice was thick and the sound loosened a knot in his stomach. Heat flooded there, south. She was right, though. He should have been asleep since he was on the next shift.

"I am. Just wanted to make sure you were okay and didn't need a hand. I'll head over there."

He got up to leave and she put a hand on his chest.

"He's okay," she said. "Sleeping and stable. You can rest for an hour or two if you need."

"Thanks. I don't know if I can, though."

She nodded. "Honestly, I'm glad you're up so it's

not so quiet. I don't love being out here alone, necessarily. Don't tell my dad when you meet him," she joked. The seriousness of her vulnerability before the last quip was a gift he hadn't thought he'd experience from her.

On top of that, she didn't chastise him, didn't tell him it was late and he'd have the next watch, and like earlier, when she'd just trusted him as a partner in the hiker's care, she was also undoing all the previous hurt his ex-wife had caused when she'd berated him for every little thing.

It hadn't always been that way in their marriage. They'd been in love once, but had started to fight over her desire to travel, to seek out something "more." *More than what?* he'd wondered. They had a beautiful little girl and a good life. Wasn't that enough? When he'd lost Allie, he'd lost his will to try—to adventure, to love, to seek out what life might offer him. He'd needed his wife, but she was all but gone by then, only her cruel words about him lingering. That he was a liability to her life of freedom, that he was a good doctor, sure, but a bore.

He'd believed her until—until the past few hours.

"Does your dad live in Hoodsport?"

She nodded, biting her lip. That she thought Reese might have the opportunity to meet the man was sweet. He wasn't sure what it meant, other than a passing comment from two people stuck in the muck of it together, but still. Add it to the list of moments he'd have to parse through when they got off this mountain.

At some point, he realized he'd dropped the *if* from the sentence. He trusted that between he and Erin, they could manage the challenge that had been presented them in the rescue, even if she hadn't been able to charge the sat phone. Damn, he wished he would have said something to his mother. He hadn't wanted to worry her, but in making that choice, he'd potentially made things infinitely worse.

Erin stretched and groaned, a noise that shot straight to his core and ignited it.

"Tell me more about him," Reese urged. Anything to distract from where his thoughts had shifted.

"He's a complicated man," she began. He didn't respond, just waited for her to continue. "When I was little, my mom left us because she couldn't handle my dad's perpetual need to chase the next adventure, the next peak, the next sunrise over a new place. She wanted a life of comfort, or at least stability, and he couldn't give her that."

It was dark, thank goodness, since he was—for some reason he couldn't fathom—turned on as hell, even in the middle of the most dangerous moment in his life. Even in the blackness, he could see the shape of her as she slid her mud-crusted pants off and slipped inside her subzero bag from the emergency supplies on the chopper. Hector was a lifesaver in more than one way. She was inches from him, their breath mingling and arms almost touching through the fabric of their separate sleep systems.

His skin buzzed with awareness.

"Or wouldn't," he added. He hated to admit it, but he understood Erin's mom's plight. He'd lived through the consequences of someone chasing those highs and the cost that came as a result. Jack-Lynn had asked him to be more of who he wasn't and had issued an ultimatum if he couldn't meet her there.

It wasn't as if he didn't want to try after Allie's death, to take walks in the easy trails of the state park, or take the ferry to one of the islands off the coast with her and Libby, in good weather. But anything more than that was asking him to sit in discomfort that bordered on pain. And for what? It wasn't enough for her. Jack-Lynn had wanted international travel to places few humans had been and he'd lost his sister to the same desire. How could he expect her to stay when he—and Libby—weren't what she wanted? She also hadn't offered to take any steps toward him and where he stood.

He'd gone to see a therapist to help with Allie's death, not knowing it would help with the loss of his family as he'd known it. He'd been devastated at the loss of Jack-Lynn at first, but in time had seen that life was better for them both if they weren't together. At that point, it was only his daughter that mattered. Somehow, combined with what he'd gone through the past few hours, he felt walls crumbling—walls he'd worked hard to build up once upon a time.

"You're right, there. He wouldn't change and she asked me to leave with her. But how could I leave the man when he was always coming home hurt? If he came home… There were nights he didn't make it back because of weather or unforeseen circumstances. My mom couldn't take it, but someone had to."

"How old were you?" he asked.

Her answer came as a whisper that was almost lost with the wind. "Eight."

He closed his eyes and hissed out a sigh.

"I don't think she knew any better. She wanted out at all costs." So had his wife, and he couldn't imagine any feeling being strong enough to leave a child behind. What an odd thing to have something in common with Erin.

"Tell me he got better, that he shaped up and became responsible for the child he was raising."

The beat of silence was heavy.

"I can't tell you that."

Reese wished he and Erin knew one another better. He'd love nothing more than to pull her into an embrace and let her know she could lay that all down. He might have been packing light, but that meant he could carry her load for a while if she would let him. He reached out of his sleep sack and found her hand. He grasped it, even though it was frigid.

"I'm so sorry."

"It's fine. I became an EMT so I could help him, and it led me to this amazing life. At the least, it allows me to explore my hometown in a different way, to be of service to the community."

He hadn't thought about it that way, that his choice to pursue medicine was a way of serving. He'd wanted to help, sure, but his community was so big, it was almost impossible to see his impact. It wasn't like he could keep in touch with his patients when they left, or post photos of them on the wall behind his desk.

His hospital saw thousands of kids per year. Tens of thousands of patients as a whole.

Erin had the luxury of seeing how her service helped others and he had to admit it was alluring. Also, like everything attached to the woman, it came with risk. She also saw the vacuum left behind when they lost one of their own. What would happen to the outpost if something happened to Hector? They'd be crushed.

"Was it your dream to become an EMT?"

"Not exactly."

"What would you have done if you could choose?" he asked. Her hand tightened in his.

"I think I would have gone to medical school. Become a surgeon. But we couldn't afford it—not the money or the time. This works for us. For me, now. It keeps me close to him."

There was a noise outside the canvas and she jolted. He held her hand close and they both listened.

"It was just the wind cracking the dry branches. We'll find some downed in the morning, I expect," she said.

"Thank you for sharing him with me," Reese said. She nodded against his shoulder, the gesture so intimate and simple it almost broke him.

"He's sick, you know."

He closed his eyes and felt her skin against his. Their fingers were interlaced and she absently rubbed the pad of his thumb. They might as well have been having sex the way he felt that small touch on every part of his body.

"I wondered about that, the way you just spoke about him. Like you're running out of time and even with his faults, he's become precious."

He felt her shift beside him and then her other hand was on top of his sleeping bag, above his chest. Her warm breath tickled the exposed skin on his neck and he smiled in spite of the seriousness of the conversation.

"Exactly. You know that, being a dad, don't you?"

Here it was, the part of his life he normally kept from everyone, lest it be used against him. The risk of opening up about Libby wasn't one he was willing to ever take on.

But he knew he could trust Erin with everything. He'd done it with his life—the rest was easy, as it turned out.

"I do."

"I love the name Libby. Is it short for Elizabeth?"

She unzipped the side of his bag and slipped her hand atop his bare chest next to one of his hands, both of them resting above his heart. He hissed as she grazed a wound he hadn't seen himself yet.

"I'm sorry. A cut?"

"I think so. One I missed when I was cleaning up in the creek, I guess." There were so many aches and pains, lacerations and bruises that they'd uncovered as the immediate danger wore off. She moved her hand south on his abdomen. He recoiled at her icy skin at the same time that desire replaced the chill. He might have been cold earlier, but that was long past. If they weren't talking about his daughter, he'd have wanted to kiss Erin again. "And her name is Olivia, actually."

"Does she share time with you both? I know you said your wife left, but how does that work for Libby?"

He shook his head and squeezed her hand.

"Nope. Her mom left us both."

"I'm so sorry you two have been through so much loss. That's why you're so worried about putting yourself at risk, isn't it? Because she's only got you?"

He nodded even though he knew she couldn't see him. "That and losing my sister. She died in a skiing accident two years ago and none of us really recovered. She was the best of us, for sure."

"That sounds so hard." Erin let a beat of silence sit between them, and in the dark, the only sounds were of their shared breathing and the wind moving through the brush. It was peaceful. "Thank you for what you're doing here, with me and for Hector. It can't be easy." No, it wasn't. But the alternative? Not being this close to Erin, not talking more deeply and more honestly than he had in his life? That wasn't tenable, either. "And I promise I'll do anything in my power to get you home to her. I'd love to see photos of you and Libby when we're back," Erin finally said.

"Of course."

He knew she meant that she'd keep him safe and get him home to Libby. And he appreciated her curiosity about Libby. He'd kept his daughter so tight to his chest, been so fearful of what sharing her might mean, that he'd neglected to think how wonderful it could be as well. Even now, it hurt to talk about her, if only because he couldn't imagine what would happen to her if they didn't survive this. Her mother had abandoned them both, but him? All he'd ever wanted was to bring her a life of abundance.

Somehow, though, sharing her with Erin doubled the feeling of joy. He'd investigate that later.

"For what it's worth," Erin said, leaning over and pressing her lips to his now-exposed shoulder, "your ex is an idiot for walking away from you."

The shock of having Erin take his side almost overrode the lingering effects of her lips on his skin.

Almost.

He turned his body so he faced her, keeping her

hand pressed to his chest despite the pressure that put on his hip that must have born the brunt of the crash. Now, being face-to-face with her, he was struck by how much he could actually see under the dim, starlit dome they'd left open to keep tabs on the weather.

Erin had pulled her bottom lip between her teeth and her gaze was pinned to his. Her eyes were wide and he had to adjust his erection in his sleeping bag as she licked her lips. She traced his collarbone from his shoulder in, then followed the curve of his neck to his jawline.

Each place she touched left a flame of want in its path, and then, before he was aware of it, her lips were pressing lightly against his.

"Is this okay?" she whispered, moving his mouth along with hers. The steam from their shared breath filled the air around them.

He nodded and tilted his head so that their lips no longer grazed one another, but were locked in a kiss. At first, it was simple, sweet, a gesture that said how she felt about him. Her lips were as soft as the rest of her was hard, and the juxtaposition made his stomach tighten with need.

When she deepened the kiss, it went from sweet to hot in an instant. Her body leaned into his and she shimmied out of her sleeping bag and wiggled into his.

He was so primally aware of Erin in his physical space. He'd seen what her hands could do when caring for someone in pain. What could she do with them to elicit pleasure?

When she reached down and found him hard and wanting her, it was all he could do to wait and let things unfold. His desire ripped through him like a shooting star.

“Is this okay?” she asked again.

“Let me make one thing clear,” he said, lifting her arms and pulling her shirt over her head. “Everything you want to do to me is okay. I’m yours.”

“Um,” she said, hesitating. He worried she’d changed her mind until she continued. “I’m on birth control, by the way. And was tested two months ago. I’m good on my end.”

He smiled. “I’m good on mine, too.”

“Then what are you doing? Get over here,” she said.

The final undoing of Reese’s resolve to stay far from risk and anything that might hurt was swift and complete. All he knew was Erin’s mouth on his, her hand cupping his strength. If by some chance they didn’t make it off the mountain, he knew he’d experienced something amazing.

And that was all he needed to give in to this woman, this moment, in case it was all he was given.

CHAPTER SEVEN

ERIN DIDN'T KNOW that she'd ever been so connected to another human. The way the two of them read each other's bodies the past three days was as if they were keys to the same lock. Or, sometimes, like he was a key unlocking parts of her she hadn't ever known existed.

The way his hands cupped her breasts and butt, as if the parts of her were precious. Then his hands would tangle in her hair when he pulled her close, as if she was the air keeping him alive on the mountain. His kisses were both deep and sensual to start, then hungry and furious as their passion increased.

Then there was the matter of the lovemaking. Holy good lover, Batman, the man could make her toes curl in all the best ways. Strong and sexy, Reese might be a bit of an indoor gym kind of guy, but he was so adept at using that strength in her favor. For instance, the night before, he'd held her above him while she rode him to the best orgasm of her life. And that became a three-peat in different positions, each one leaving her more sated and fulfilled than she'd ever been.

That wasn't all, either.

He'd cuddled her until she'd fallen asleep the past two nights, then he'd taken her shift and his, back to back. She'd awoken on day three, maybe not fully refreshed, but the most she'd been since they'd crashed.

She'd had good sex before when she was lonely and found an attractive traveler that was passing through and also in want of a night with company. But there was something so different about this.

Because it's not just sex.

Maybe not. It was the shared trauma, for sure.

And…her heart pressed her.

Sure. She had a glaring crush on the guy. Being cared for in the ways he cared for her was addicting and wholly crush-generating. Not a good combo when she couldn't count on any of her friends—Lila, for example—to slap some sense into her. No, it was keeping Hector alive and healing, stealing small moments of pleasure when they could, and hoping she didn't fall further for him, or…

The alternative was the one thing they were trying to avoid.

So, good, mind-blowing sex to stave off existential terror it was. If a harmless crush was a side effect, then so be it. It was worth it, short as their time together was—their real mission was Hector.

Speaking of…

His pain consistently woke him in the middle of the night, meaning either she or Reese would spend half the night caring for him. All of them were barely getting by.

That part of the unexpected detour from home was as miserable as anyone could imagine, even without juxtaposing it against her stolen bliss. They did their best to keep Hector fed and hydrated, saving the soups for him since liquids were all they could get in his mouth most meals. Water was the same process—force opening his mouth and hoping he didn't gag on the liquid as it passed down his throat. They had enough of both it seemed, but they were only on day three of being stranded. Water would keep—they'd discovered the stream was more than plentiful and safe to drink. But food was an altogether different story.

Reese had gone berry picking after she'd taught him what to look for and come back with some mountain blackberriess and blueberries that were at the end of their life. It replenished their depleting bounty. Erin didn't think she could catch a fish in the upper mountain stream, but supposed that was an option. What else was there?

Keeping up with Hector's basic needs was hard, but keeping him comfortable was impossible.

"What are we going to do with him today?" Reese asked her that afternoon, kissing her on the cheek as he sat beside her at their campfire. He'd started becoming more affectionate with her outside their canvas shelter, which was nice, but also confusing.

What were they, if not people bound together by

tragedy who were attracted to one another? Sure, she liked him, had a schoolgirl crush on the man, but starting something real with him wasn't possible. Not really.

She'd accept what she could get out here, though. Who knew what the future had in store for them, and she'd be damned if she wasted a second of it not *living*. Including kissing the handsome man beside her. The juxtaposition between that and the terror when Hector would cry out at night was fraying her nerves, but they were destroyed after the crash, anyway. At least Reese gave her something to *hope* for.

Reese rubbed his hands together before taking hers and putting them on his lap. The rain had abated, but the open skies had let the heat escape, so now the fire was necessary for warmth as well.

"I'm not sure. We can keep up with our normal protocol, but I think we need to start ambulatory movements so his circulatory system doesn't shut down. He looks—"

"Bad," Reese offered. He wasn't wrong. Hector's eyes had dark black circles under them, and his skin was pale and clammy. He needed medical attention—the right kind of sterile, constant medical attention that could only be found in a medical facility—immediately. "I'll work on it while I'm on shift. It's part of my protocol for paraplegic and quadriplegic patients."

"Thanks," Erin said. She leaned her head on his

shoulder and he tilted her chin until their lips met. Like it always did, his kiss felt like heat straight from the source, like…comfort in human form.

She melted into it until Hector cried out.

They both shot up. "I'll grab him," she said at the same time Reese said, "I've got the kit."

They were still a good team, even if this routine of saving Hector only to sit in fear he'd decompensate again in a few hours was the clock they set their watches by. How much more was sustainable for any of them?

Erin put her wrist on Hector's forehead, which was clammier than before. He was burning up.

"His fever's worsened," she said as Reese hung a Ziploc bag of antibiotics. They'd crushed the pills and added them to saline, then used a clean sandwich sack as a hanging med bag.

"Do we know why?" Reese asked. She shook her head.

"His wound looks clean, if not a little raw still. But no heat. There's got to be something going on beneath the surface."

"You look like you're considering something," he said. She was, but it was only an idea she'd gotten from reading the medical journals she secretly sent to the office. "I trust you."

She twisted her lips into a half smile. "For what it's worth, I wouldn't. I'm an EMT who reads too much, but…"

"Lay it on me. We've got to figure this out, Erin."

"I think we need to search for a clot. I've read about this in *The New England Journal of Medicine*."

Reese's face lit up. "I read that article, too. Wait…how'd you get your hands on that?"

Erin felt like she was the one with the high temperature the way heat spread across her skin. "Um, I—"

"You buy your own copies, don't you?" She nodded. "We're coming back to that, but right now, I think that's a good bet. I'll get an instrument that might work."

Erin grabbed his hand on the way out of the tent. "Thank you, Reese. For trusting me."

"Always," he said, and was gone again. While he gathered the extra supplies they'd need, Erin cleaned the dressing on Hector's incision and talked to him the way she always did when she was on shift. He didn't always answer, but it was impossible to imagine ignoring their friendship any longer. He was a patient, yes, but he'd been a medic family member for so much longer.

Now, that was the thing that mattered most.

"Hey, buddy. Just thinking about how we met. Remember you spilled your coffee all down my new medic hoodie?" She laughed, and wiped away a stray tear at the memory. "Gosh, you were such a baby back then, so young and hotheaded. I think you met Dee the next week, didn't you?"

She washed his forehead with a wet bandanna and he shivered. He'd never really regained consciousness, but he was in there somewhere, fighting off whatever was trying to kill him. Erin was almost a hundred-percent sure it was a clot, specifically around his wound. She'd have to open him back up to see. It was a risky move, but the way he'd deteriorated said bold moves were necessary.

"She wasn't even jealous of our friendship, just walked right up to me and said she liked you, recognized you and I were close, and that she wasn't going to let that get in the way of being with you, or her and I becoming friends. I don't think I've ever been as impressed by a woman's boldness before."

"I have," Reese said. Erin sat back on her heels. "There's a woman I know who not only jumped off the side of a cliff, but put a chest tube in a man with a collapsed lung in the middle of the forest. She's amazing."

"I didn't hear you come back," she whispered. "And that kind of bravery is just adrenaline. It's nothing special because everyone has it."

"Oh, I know. I wasn't done. That same woman cares so much for her father and friends and has helped me ease my own insecurities by talking to me every night and opening up to me even though we've both been hurt by people before. That kind of bravery is quiet, but so strong." He took her hands in his. "I hope she sees that and acknowledges how amazing she is."

Erin felt the tears that had begun when she'd started talking to Hector fall freely on her cheeks now. Those were maybe the kindest words anyone had ever spoken to her. So why were they so hard to believe?

"Thanks, Reese. I'm—I'm getting there. Did you find anything that would work?"

"Believe it or not, I did." He held up a green, wide-mouth straw. "And it was the one useful thing that came from my bag."

She laughed at the joke they'd shared since Reese's bag was found to be, well, less than helpful when it came to actual supplies they'd need outside a backyard camping excursion.

"Oh, hush. We've used that cotton hoodie you brought," she said, gesturing to the makeshift pillow beneath Hector's head. Reese laughed deeply, one of the absolute greatest sounds she thought she'd ever heard, if not because of its rarity.

"Okay, well, you ready to do this?" She nodded, even though she wasn't sure she was. Hector was back to being a patient, a man with a family on the other side.

They all had families on the other side of the operating room.

Yes, but Dee had tossed Erin her bouquet at her wedding. This family was about to grow by one and Erin was invested in helping Hector meet his daughter.

"Keep talking to him," Reese urged.

"But last time you said—"

"Last time, Hector was going to die in minutes without care. Right now, he needs to know what he's fighting to stay alive for. Keep talking and

I'll take this one, okay? You don't have to do this alone."

Erin's chest might have caved in at that last sentence if she could withstand any more pain.

"Thank you," she whispered. She started talking to Hector, as Reese instructed. "You hear that? You've got a lot to fight to stay alive for. Me, for one. I have so many stories to tell you and jokes I thought of that you'd find hilarious." She'd tried for funny and lighthearted but it wasn't how she really felt. "More than that, you've got Dee. She loves you so much and has built such a beautiful life for you two. I never told you this, but six months ago, maybe just before you guys found out you were pregnant, she brought me lunch at work. I told her you were on a flight and she said she knew, that she'd been worried because she texted you the superstitious thing she always did before a flight but found out it was after you took off."

Reese glanced up at her just after opening up the top of Hector's incision. Blood pooled almost immediately. She wiped it to clear the way for Reese to explore for clots.

"Keep going," Reese urged her.

She could barely see through her tears, but they didn't matter—couldn't matter, not when Hector was literally fighting to stay alive. What right did she have to cry when she wasn't the one with something to lose, the one on the table being opened up?

You have something to lose.

Maybe. She couldn't think about that, either. She

and Reese would—maybe? Hopefully?—have time to figure out their…whatever they were doing. But it involved more than them. He had Libby and that meant the pieces shifted.

"Hector, she was so worried that day because she loves you so much. I know you got back and told her she was silly, that no special ritual was going to make up for more luck than your years of flight time gave you, but I think her ritual was her way of controlling the uncontrollable. Also, it was her way of saying 'I love you.' That's kind of beautiful, isn't it?"

"I found the clot," Reese said, digging it out with the straw and discarding it in the tin cup they'd designated as a waste bin in the makeshift surgical space. "There's two, actually."

"He's going to keep throwing them without the proper medical care. Which means he's at risk for—"

"A stroke. I know." He sighed and dug out the second clot, then worked to close the wound again. His jaw was set tight. "Where the hell is a rescue chopper? A hiking team? Anyone. He needs to get out of here like yesterday."

She'd wondered the same thing for a while now… They all needed to get out of there. Their nerves were frayed, their health deteriorating.

Hope was waning, as were their medical supplies at this point.

Why hadn't they been found yet? Lila would know they'd crashed. Reese's mom, not hearing from him for days now, would have sent word to the authorities, right?

Her father… She choked on a sob as she wondered what was going on with him. He had his own medical worries, but they'd become her fears as well.

Please let him be okay, she prayed to whoever or whatever might be listening. They seemed more isolated and alone than ever.

They cleaned up and left Hector sleeping off the stress of the surgery. They needed to eat and rest, feel human again. They were both so tightly wound, they were liable to snap at any point.

When they'd recentered, then they could get back to rotations.

"Can I ask you something?" he asked her as they warmed up the second-to-last MRE. After this, it was soup, berries, and water. Not exactly the menu at a Ritz-Carlton, but hopefully enough until…

She didn't want to think about that. She had to keep hope they'd be rescued or find their own way out.

"Anything." They'd grown so close over the past few days, she couldn't imagine him bringing up something she wouldn't want to discuss with him.

"Have you thought of going to med school?"

Okay, except maybe that.

She felt the heat on her cheeks from the embarrassment that cropped up every time someone asked her something similar. Shame was attached to that particular wound.

She wasn't where she wanted to be in life, not really. The clinic and its planning were her way of staving off the guilt at not pursuing her own dreams while she worked to let her father live his.

The irony that she was the child and that was his role, as Reese had pointed out, wasn't lost on her. That shame she carried each day as she worked to help others make their dreams come true, even if her role was just making sure they lived another day.

At least there was honor in that…

She forced herself to look him in the eyes.

"Yes. I did at one point. When I was a little girl, my friends were so annoyed with me—it's the only game I ever wanted to play. Wanna know something funny?" He nodded. There was something so welcoming about the gentle way he asked questions, because he wanted the answer and let her keep talking because he seemed to want to learn more about her. "I started a doctor's office in the forest, where I would have my friends come when they were hurt. I stocked it with bandages and acetaminophen I stole from the outpost. I even think I had a stethoscope up there. I made my friends call me Dr. Erin for months. No wonder they all grew up and left."

"I don't know that your passion for medicine is what made them seek out new horizons, unless it was because you had the courage to follow your dreams and they wanted to try that for themselves. Maybe you inspired them."

Erin frowned. She hadn't thought about it that way. Except… She hadn't followed her dreams, not really. She'd ridden the current of events happening to and around her, and not stopped to think if this was the river that would take her to where she wanted to be.

"What happened to that office?" he asked. "Seems like a good plan with all the injuries up here."

He winked and the insides of her all seemed to switch places.

"Touché. But, yeah. If I'm honest, that's what made me think of it all these years later. As for the original clinic? My dad caught me and made me return all the stuff I stole. Six years later, Lila offered me a job as an assistant until I was old enough to get my EMT license. Said she knew then I'd be a helluva medic. Kinda funny how life works out, huh?"

Medicine had always been a part of her life, like adventure was a part of her father's. Now, her dad relied on her help and medical care. All she hoped was that he was okay with her gone. That he hadn't had a flare-up.

If she got home and found him—

No. She couldn't go there. Reese wrapped an arm around her. How did he know when her thoughts had gone dark? Every single time, he reassured her with a touch or embrace.

He knew more about her than anyone other than Lila, and he'd only known her a few days. *Yeah, but a few days of intensity. It's like a crash course in getting to know someone. Pun not intended,* her snarky subconscious cackled.

"It is, but I just like to think it's worked out so far. Why haven't you gone back to school since? It seems like it was so important to you."

It had been. And he was right. Why hadn't she? That current had been too strong, or at least that's how she recalled it. It didn't matter, anyway. She'd been deposited on a river beach and this was her life now.

"It's futile—I'm too old and too needed at my job. Besides, I'm happy as an EMT."

He raised his eyebrows and mouthed *bullsh—*

Those were all things she believed, and yet… they were only part of the story. Reese didn't drop her gaze, and suddenly, it was as if the sun came out and heat poured over her.

"I told Libby the other day that being happy was different than being content when she said her mean, bully of a friend at day care made her happy." Erin froze. He hadn't mentioned Libby much since they crashed. "I tried to share that she actually just didn't want to lose something she was used to. She didn't understand a damn thing I was saying, but I'll pose that to you now. Are you actually happy and fulfilled, or is the version of you trying to build a clinic the part that wanted to be a doctor coming out?"

Heat built behind her eyes. "I don't know."

"You don't have to decide now. Just know it's

never too late to pursue your dreams." He kissed her on the cheek again and went to check on Hector for his shift.

She let his statement wash over her as she walked to the creek to literally wash the day off her. The blood from Hector's clot mixed with the grime from the hiking and other tasks she'd had to do to keep up the camp.

Her legs were so sore that the water felt good.

Every day, she pushed farther out to see if she could reach someone on the sat phone, with its waning battery that wouldn't hold a charge, even though she'd found a way to hook it up to the helicopter's transistor. No luck so far. It wasn't enough.

She mulled his question over while she bathed.

"I think I should try to make it out," she told him that night as they lay together after dinner. They gave themselves an hour together when Hector slept off his dinner and meds. It was the best part of her day, for sure, but honestly, she thought she'd feel that way even if they weren't stranded in the mountains. She genuinely liked Reese's company, a cataclysmic shift from their first meeting. She smiled in spite of the seriousness of the conversation she'd brought up. "I don't see a way out of this that doesn't include one of us leaving for help."

Reese's gazc was pinned on the crease in the canvas above them and his fingers ran lazy circles on Erin's arm.

"I don't think we should separate," he said. She was glad he couldn't see her smile. She was well aware—more like absolutely certain—that he hadn't meant it as anything more than the fact that they should stay at camp with their patient, but still.

It was nice to daydream that they were off this mountain and she could curl up in an actual bed with this man. The reality was sharper.

"I'm just worried we won't find help."

"Me, too. I'm just as worried something will happen to you and you won't have me—or, well, anyone—to help you. Call me crazy, but I think our best chances of success will be staying together and waiting this out."

She nodded against his shoulder, worry and hope warring for space in her chest cavity.

It was a question she needed to think about for sure. Making the wrong choice could hurt them all, even prove fatal. But how could they know what that was, unless something happened to work out?

That was the big, existential question looming over everything, wasn't it? It addressed Reese's question about medical school and what she was doing next. When he'd asked her, he'd squeezed her hand when she said she'd looked into programs in the city.

Don't read into it.

She wasn't, but what would her future look like, if she dared to dream? Aside from the obvious, that she could maybe have her daydream come true—curling up with Reese in an actual bed—she could give her inner child what she'd always wanted.

A medical degree and the chance to be a doctor.

And the other thing was nice, too, though as she thought through both options, she realized she had a better chance of getting a medical degree than she did making a relationship work with her schedule and lifestyle. She had tried long and hard to convince people—anyone, really—to stick around, and no one had.

Not her mother, not her best friend, not her first serious boyfriend during college, Ben. They'd all left for…more.

She wanted to ask more about Reese's life, more about his daughter, but each time she did, he told her it was too hard to picture her when he needed to survive, he said.

"I think about her every second of every day," he'd told her, his eyes vacant and distant. The point was, Erin wasn't invited in, not yet.

Reese lives in the city with his daughter, her subconscious added. *He has "more" already. Why would he want to trade that for less?*

She didn't think her life was less; how could it be, surrounded by the trees and mountains and elk and bear and…

No, this life was plenty big enough—too big sometimes—and anyone who didn't see that wasn't someone she wanted to be with, anyway.

Could he want that? Could they give up what they have to live out here with me? A good question for a thought study, but one thing got in the way of her seeing the daydream to fruition…

They had to survive being rescued first.

CHAPTER EIGHT

REESE'S ARMS BURNED under the exertion of carrying the logs back to the fire. He'd built a certain strength in the gym—partly for vanity reasons, like a lot of his friends, and partly to make sure he could keep up with Libby and also be the best doctor he could, health-wise.

What he needed to survive out here required a different kind of stamina than anything else he'd trained for. It was also making him into a muscle-powered machine, even just shy of a week in.

Sure, hauling logs wasn't the norm, unless a person was camping or lived rurally and had to collect logs for keeping warm each winter—part of why he lived in the city with central heat—but it was better than kettlebell swings for building his raw power, that was for sure.

He deposited the logs by the fire, noting that they'd need kindling, too. Erin was changing Hector's bandages, so he headed back out to grab an armful of sticks. Everything was a little damp, but in keeping the wood near the never-ceasing fire, it did help in drying out what they'd need for the next round.

They had a system down at this point, but it was getting stale. He was a man who thrived on routine, but this situation was pushing those limits.

He ate a few berries while he gathered a pile to bring back, the juices once new and exciting to his taste buds now as muted as the weather, which had gotten worse again.

Reese thought about what Erin said about ritual and…love. He wasn't quite there with her—how could he be, when they'd only known one another for a week? But it didn't mean they hadn't developed real feelings for one another as they'd navigated their crisis.

Their rituals were grounded in daily tasks, in caring for Hector, in loving one another each night. How would that shift if—no, he chastised himself, when—they were rescued?

Were they only able to connect and overcome their differences because everything else was voided by their circumstances? Or was the connection they were forming out here showing them what they could do together if they put aside those differences back home?

You're asking the wrong questions.

What does she want? Does she want you? None of this matters if she isn't ready for anything else.

That was true, and he'd make sure to ask her. Eventually. Right now, it was back to the rituals.

Stoke fire, eat, meds to Hector, bathe in the creek, make love, sleep. Wake up and repeat.

His arms were scratched up from the twigs and branches he'd foraged, meaning he might be switching up the ritual just a bit by bathing first. Ugh. He needed a change of scenery, of pace.

He tossed the sticks on top of the logs and prepared to add some of each to the fire, when Erin walked up the path they'd made to the creek. Her hair was wet and draped over a shoulder, her toned, strong arms exposed and dappled with moisture.

The small camp towel she'd brought in her day pack did little to cover curves he'd traced with his fingers and tongue, but somehow was sexier than seeing her naked beneath him.

Well, maybe. It was a toss-up.

"Hi," she whispered, when she caught him staring. Her voice was thick and shot straight to his core. And south. He adjusted his hiking pants to accommodate the effects she had on him.

"Sorry," he said, moving to meet her. "I didn't mean to stare. But you're—you're beautiful."

Her smile was the one saving grace around there. Without it, he'd have had some pretty dark moments.

"You can stare all day if that's the result."

"It's not the only result..." He sheepishly removed his hands from what they'd attempted to cover. His erection pressed against his pants, proof of his feelings for her.

"We should take advantage of that, shouldn't we?"

He smiled. This was just the change to their routines he needed. He needed Erin. With increasing frequency, as fate would have it.

"I mean, it would be irresponsible to let anything die out here, especially a hard-on that could give so much back to..." He waved over the length of her. "To the community."

She laughed and crooked a finger. "As a doctor, I know you promised to do no harm, so, Dr. Vallen, I'm going to need you to use that instrument for pleasure instead. Code blue," she teased.

His laugh rang out across camp. He'd never been efficacious with his joy, had considered himself content, if not happy. But somehow, here, in the terror of their situation, he'd found joy, too.

They'd stolen each moment where there'd been a break in the constant shift of responsibility—caring for Hector, keeping the fire alive, walking to find help, keeping food on the makeshift table, to name a few—to love one another.

Erin made it possible and he'd never be anything less than grateful he'd met her, even under those circumstances.

He carried that gratitude, along with her naked self, since her towel now hung on the line outside, into the tent.

He laid her atop the sleeping bags they'd long ago zipped together to make one sleeping system they could share. The look in her eyes as he grazed his fingers along her silhouette was pure want and fire.

Her skin erupted in gooseflesh where he touched,

so he followed the path with his tongue and lips. As he suspected would happen, warmth blossomed, driving away the chill on her skin.

"I love how every cell in your body shows me what you like. You don't need to tell me a thing." He took off his shirt so he could feel her bare skin against his.

Reese paused his expedition at the apex of her thighs and took a detour he'd been wanting to explore more, into her soft warm folds.

"Oh…" she said. "I—"

"You can talk to me if you think I'm doing something wrong, or you want something more," he teased. Her body reacted by bucking her hips, drawing him in. "That's my girl," he whispered against her sex.

She purred with uninhibited desire. "More," she begged.

He obliged.

She was so wet for him, and he used his tongue to taste her, to invite her brine to be part of his palette. He didn't need four-star restaurants if he could dine on this all day, every day.

He didn't mind the risk if he could explore her as his reward. She was getting healthier, too. Her bruises were healing, her cuts closing. His were, too. His internal wounds as well. She was responsible for that, too.

Erin moaned, her fists tangled in his hair. He dived deeper, sucking and pulling until her thighs pressed together, trapping him there inside her. Oh, he could die there, trapped for eternity a happy man.

"Reese," she rasped. They'd tried to keep their trysts quiet, a sin as far as he was concerned, given the almost-complete solitude they were surrounded by. He considered it the only perk to being out here at all. But Hector's health mattered more than their shared passion. Somehow, in the moment, though, making their voices heard felt imperative. "I'm close."

"Come for me," he urged, slipping two fingers inside her while he sucked on her sensitive bud.

In seconds, her body was in spasms, a cry of pleasure ripping through their tent, and camp, and probably the whole valley.

She kissed his chest, peppering him with her soft lips while her body calmed. Her eyes, though, held the same wantonness as before.

"Your turn," she said. Her voice was husky and familiar. His erection jumped to attention, his body a divining rod where her touch was concerned as well. She sat up and straddled him, her moist sex still glistening with them both.

Damn, she was the sexiest thing he'd ever seen.

When she undid his zipper, he sprang free and her eyes lit up. Okay, that was the sexiest thing he'd ever seen. She wanted him, and he craved her in return.

When she bent over him, her damp hair tickling his taut abdomen, her mouth on his shaft, he nearly came then and there. But he waited, allowing the singular pleasure of her tongue sliding across his tip, her mouth sucking on all he gave her while her hand rode him in tandem.

"Good g—" he blurted when she increased the pressure and speed, her breasts grazing his thighs. The rest of his proclamation died in his throat and came out as a deep growl of approval.

She was incredible.

He felt the building pressure low in his groin and she must have noticed because she gave a subtle nod. He let the release happen and could barely keep control when she swallowed him whole, never letting up while he shivered against her. The orgasm lasted what seemed like minutes, the only sound her sated breathing that matched his ragged breaths.

That, and the crackle of the fire outside. Night had slipped in while they made love and he pulled her up to rest her head on his shoulder, but not before kissing her so he could taste them on her lips.

"Well, that was one way to pass an evening out here," he whispered into her hair. "You know, if you keep that up, I might just find out I enjoy hiking and camping."

She laughed, her breath warm on his exposed skin. "Yeah, I'm rethinking my own position on that, given our current circumstances. I'm actually thinking how much fun that'll be when we have an actual bed to do it in."

He squeezed her tight against him and tried not

to let the heaviness of what she was really saying impact the joy they'd just shared.

But she'd mentioned two of his fears. One, that they wouldn't get that chance because rescue seemed too far off to fathom. The other that she wouldn't share that feeling if they did make it back. Their whole partnership was so tenuous, like the rest of their fate.

She started to get up, to find her clothes, but he pulled her back down.

"C'mere," he said. "Linger with me a little." She nodded lazily and he knew she was as exhausted as he felt.

Sure enough, in seconds she'd started snoring softly. He let her sleep and just traced her skin and hair with his fingertips, enjoying the moment.

"It's cold," she whispered into his arm sometime later. He could tell from her voice she was still half wrapped in sleep. So was he. *Damn.* "We should get in the bag." At some point they both must've fallen asleep, but he couldn't recall the moment her light snores had given way to his own. But sure enough, there was a hint of sun peeking over the horizon.

Goodness knew they both needed the rest.

"We are in the bag, babe," he murmured. "Give me half an hour until we get up, please. I'm so happy with my little body pillow nuzzled against me, keeping me warm." She sat up like she'd been bitten and he begrudgingly opened his eyes. "What's up? You okay, Erin?"

She shook her head violently and got out of the

bag, then threw on the clothes she'd just taken off the line. The creek had kept them and their clothes clean in addition to hydrating them all week. Wherever the source of water was from, Reese was grateful for it.

"Erin, talk to me."

"The fire. It's out."

He shook his head, ran a hand through his hair, feeling sand at the base of it. "No," he said. "I brought back logs and kindling like usual. I—"

The rest of the sentence hung in midair like the remnants of the smoke from the fire that was supposed to be so much more than a source of warmth. It was supposed to be their way out of there.

"You what? Tell me you added logs to the fire, too. Reese, please tell me—"

He threw on pants and his shirt, tugged on his boots without socks, and sprinted out of the tent. Sure enough, where the fire had been raging for six days now, there was only a cold pile of ash with small tendrils of smoke rising up, instead of the hundred-foot-high tower of it that had been present all week.

"No," he whispered.

"What did you do?" she asked. His nerves—still frayed from before—flared up.

He pointed at his chest. "Me?"

"Yes, you. This…" She walked around the campfire, frantically gathering any stick that looked dry enough and tossing it on the dying embers. "This was your responsibility. I'm on top of hiking each day, and you've got the fire, remember?" He did remember. He'd taken on so many things that were out of his comfort zone and handled them well. This was an accident.

He took a deep breath, steadying his own fears and insecurities. This wasn't about him, not really. His therapist, helping through the aftermath of Allie's death so he could go back to practicing medicine, had talked to him about people's reasons for lashing out. He'd been struggling to understand the last thing Allie had said to him—that he needed to live life to the fullest and let others do the same.

His therapist had exhorted that "people claw at whatever is in front of them when they're in pain. It isn't always about the person taking the brunt of the wrath—in fact, most of the time, it isn't."

Erin was scared, just like he was. She was hungry and tired and overstimulated. Just like he was.

You're not lashing out at her, though.

He wasn't, but who was to say if she'd messed up about something vital to their rescue that he wouldn't have done the same thing?

"Thank you for rebuilding it," he said. There wasn't much grace evident in his voice to match the words, but it was the best he could do at the moment. "I'll go walk our morning perimeter and see what I can find. For what it's worth, I'm sorry. I know this is devastating."

"Reese..." she said. She didn't close the gap between them, but there was reticence in her gaze.

"Yeah?" She'd been angry and scared. He would

forgive her—of course, he would. Especially with the apology that was on her lips. Even that was so different from Jack-Lynn, who would have found a way to make him feel even worse. "You can talk to me, Erin."

"I know." The edge was back in her voice. "I just didn't know if you knew the way around the edge of the camp. We can't have you getting lost, on top of everything else."

He grimaced.

"Got it. I'll do my best, but I'm not the outdoor human you are."

Gone was his patience, his willingness to apologize. If it was going to be one-sided, he could sling barbs, too.

Except they didn't feel good at all to fire off at her, even if they might've been deserved. She might not have been kind about it, but she hadn't been wrong. He'd gotten better, stronger, but he still could be considered a certain liability out here that someone her equal wouldn't.

That fanned the flames of a worry he'd had since he'd developed the crush on her. What did she see in him besides a warm body to keep her company in what was the worst moment in either of their lives? His impostor syndrome set in hard, crashing against him like a rogue wave off the coast.

He was a city doctor, a man who thrived with structure and routine and, yeah, the safety of creature comforts like a city-block-wide grocery store with an assortment of wines and cheeses he could choose from for dinners. Like parking near where he needed to go so he could avoid the elements, or if he couldn't, outerwear that helped shield his Brooks Brothers suit from getting wet.

Of course, he didn't know how to handle Erin, to keep up with her.

She was wild and free, a feral woman with an untethered heart. He liked her for it, too. Who was he to try and rein in something as beautiful as her spirit?

She needed someone who not only understood her, which he felt he could safely say he was, but who also could join her. Encourage her. Support her.

Maybe it was better they'd had this little spat now, when they could start to separate their emotions for each other from the trauma bond that had united them in the first place.

Do you really believe that's all this is? A psychological thread tied between you?

No, he didn't, but what did it matter?

They were too different, from two different worlds that were more than oceans apart. Hell, they might as well be from different solar systems. She wasn't like Jack-Lynn, but one thing he'd learned since his ex-wife had left him? He wasn't going to convince anyone of his worth. They either saw it and how it could add to their life, or they didn't.

He rounded a corner that threw the path due east and came to a grinding halt. A black bear stood before him, a small cub at the base of the berry bush beside her.

"Hey there," he said, his voice strong and firm. His insides were a different story. They bucked and tossed like he was aboard a deep-sea vessel in a storm. This was too wild for him, no question. "I'm just gonna back up and head back the way I came."

He'd have failed at completing the task he'd taken on to help them—his second failure in a day—but what choice did he have? He wasn't going to risk his life to walk a perimeter on the off chance there was an errant hiker out there. He hoped Erin would do the same thing—protect herself first, at all costs, even their freedom.

He stepped back slowly, in awe of the massive beast and small cub that were just there, no worries about food or shelter or their place in anyone's lives.

When he was sure they weren't going to chase after him, he jogged back to Erin, another apology ready on his lips.

She met him at the back side of camp and wrapped him in an unexpected embrace.

"I'm sorry," she whispered against his chest. "I was just worried."

His hands tangled in her hair, forgiveness and care already washing away any negative thoughts he'd had about her or them being together. This was all that mattered to him, that they continued to grow together, however slowly. He pulled back, though, and told her about the bears.

"They're beautiful, aren't they?" she asked.

"You've seen them?"

She nodded. "Every day. They wander the path a different way each time, so I have to pivot and find a new way through. But pivoting isn't bad, you know. When we have new information, we're allowed to change course."

He smiled. "Very wise advice for dealing with…" He paused and kissed her. "Bears."

"Mmm-hmm. I'm brilliant, remember? I think you said it—"

He tickled her, enjoying her squeal of delight. Then he grew serious. "How's Hector? I really am so sorry. And I'll seriously pivot and go the other way on the path just to check."

"Hector is okay. He warmed up once the fire was roaring again. I'd venture a guess we only lost an hour without any smoke, so hopefully it's okay. But it's not your fault any more than something horrible happening to Hector would be mine. We're both operating on limited energy and wits at this point."

"Literally operating," he teased. She giggled.

"Yeah, true. Anyway, I'm sorry, too. I was scared to lose you, Reese. I was about to apologize, but then you were telling me how you'd take on a chore for me as your own mea culpa and I just… I felt so bad. Not only for how I spoke to you, which was abysmal."

"It was," he said. He kissed her as his own form of punctuation on that small gentle chiding. "But I've got tougher skin than you realize."

"I know. It's so wrapped up in why I care about

you so deeply. You're able to grow and change, and you're inspiring me to do the same. Anyway, I felt bad because if I lost you when I had just said such horrible words to you, I'd never forgive myself."

He understood that. He'd been so cruel to Allie and vice versa that last day before she'd died. An unspoken apology would always float above him like a buoy just out of reach. He'd drown trying to keep going after it.

"I'm fine, and we will be, too, Erin. I still believe that."

He meant more than just safe. He meant they would have time to figure out their relationship once the safety part had been settled.

"I do, too."

"What do we do now?" he asked. Her eyes got wide, and they were adorable paired with her red cheeks and sheepish grin. "I mean that sounds good, too, but I was thinking about Hector, food, and the perimeter walk."

"Let's start with my idea and handle the rest later?"

For two people who'd been overly responsible their whole lives—especially lately—it seemed like a rash choice.

On the other hand, what did they have to lose? In the face of everything falling apart, clinging to one another seemed a good way to go.

"I'll follow you anywhere," he told her. The way she leaned into him confirmed that sentiment. But was it actually not his gift to give, the promise that he'd always be there.

Worry followed him into the tent this time.

He cared about this woman and anything close to losing her wasn't anything he was willing to negotiate.

The problem was, she wasn't the only woman in his life. His daughter was his first priority, something easy to forget when survival in the woods was the key to seeing her again.

Real life seemed so far away from them at the moment—too far. But it also crept dangerously close. The more they wished for rescue, the more he realized how much would change when it came.

He wasn't prepared for that, so it made sense that being with Erin was the only thing he could concentrate on. Like he'd been repeating since they crashed. Who knew how much time they really had left?

CHAPTER NINE

ERIN HAD BEEN awake for probably half an hour, the waning supplies on her mind. Should she set up traps? What would they catch up there but maybe a squirrel or bird. Neither would last long with three people. It was probably better for her to forage for early chanterelles and more berries. As long as she could avoid the mom-cub bear duo, that was.

Something cracked outside, drawing her attention to more immediate things. It was more than just a branch splitting. And it was close.

Erin stilled her breathing. She distinctly heard the crunching of leaves outside their campsite and sat up, alert despite the hint of orange on the horizon indicating there were still hours before full daylight.

Six days. More than half a week.

She slid silently out of the joint sleeping bag she shared with Reese, leaving him in what looked like a peaceful sleep. At the entrance to the tent, she snatched the bear spray they kept handy.

"Who's out there?" she asked. She knew for a fact it was a human, based on the patterns of the footfalls. She'd done too many rescues in the wilderness to mistake the animals she encountered. By her estimation, there were more than two men and they were within sight distance.

Damn the light that time of year. Mornings were as lazy as a cat in the sun.

"Hello?" she asked again, pointing the bear spray at the head of the campsite, where the trail intersected it. "I am prepared to fight," she added. Her stomach clenched at the idea. How would she and Reese protect Hector?

"I kinda hope you don't do that," a man said, coming through the clearing. The first thing she noticed was how tall—and clean—he was. As were the two men behind him. They all came to the clearing with their hands held high in the air as if they were doing a perp walk.

"We come in peace," the second said. "You're the one keeping the fire day and night, right?" he asked.

She nodded, her throat thick.

"Freaking finally," the third guy said. "Can I put my hands down?"

Erin nodded again, even though she had no idea who these guys were. All she could trust was that her intuition—her greatest gift as a medic—was keyed in right now, too.

"I'm Ian," the first man said, reaching to shake her hand. "This is my brother, Greg," he said, pointing to the third guy with a scowl on his face like they'd ruined his day by being there. "That's our friend, Ethan."

"Nice to meet you," she said. "I'm Erin, an EMT. We had a flight medic accident and are stranded. Are you in any condition to help us get off the mountain? We have one injured man and a pediatric surgeon who is healthy, but we can't move the patient."

Ian laughed, though Erin couldn't see what was funny.

"Um, yeah, we can help. We're all surgeons and mountaineers and we've been tracking your location for two and a half days."

Greg hit his brother. "How's the patient?"

Erin let out a sob. They had help. Not just help, either, but the kind that could actually get them home safe and whole.

"He's in bad shape, but stable. Can I show you?"

Greg nodded, and Ethan came over to her, his gaze flitting between her and the wreckage at the edge of camp.

"How are *you*? That looks like a helluva crash."

A hand pressed against her lower back, centering her. She inhaled and leaned into it.

"We're fine," she said, moving closer to Reese. She hadn't seen or heard him come out. "We were in the back and got some minor cuts and bruises. Miraculously, nothing more."

"Shit. I'd say." Ethan picked up Erin's arm and looked as amazed as she felt knowing they'd made it almost unscathed.

"You're here to help?" Reese asked. She nodded, along with the men.

"Greg, Ian, and—" she said, pointing to the third man.

"Ethan. Nice to meet you, man. Judging by how mobile you are, I'm guessing you're the pediatric surgeon?" He took off his pack and began readying supplies that they hadn't had access to. A saline bag, meds… It was amazing, and brought tears to her eyes.

Reese nodded.

"We were telling your partner we've been following your smoke for two days now, figuring anyone who wasn't moving that far in, and who was keeping the fire going in these daytime temps, was in trouble. We're just glad you two are okay. We worried when we got to the ravine and had to find a way to bypass it that we'd be too late."

"We're close with our third," Reese said.

"We're all surgeons, as well, so put us to work," Ian added.

Erin was still reeling from having help here that she almost missed them call Reese her partner. It unnerved her, but somehow…fit. After all, weren't they just that, for all intents and purposes, the past six days as they cared for themselves and Hector?

Reese barked out a laugh. "Well, hell. When help comes, it comes with bells on, huh? Follow me. I'll fill you in about Hector, our flight captain who was injured when we crashed, and ask you to weigh on how to make him movable. Pneumothorax and some other impact-related injuries." He turned back. "And thanks, guys. This is literally life-saving."

"Happy to help," Ethan said.

"Yeah, but next time try and crash closer to the main campsite," Greg said. Everyone laughed, the mood at the campsite decidedly cheerier than it had been.

Ethan added, "I can't believe you guys kept a guy with a pneumothorax alive in the field. This I gotta see."

The three docs followed Reese into the med tent and she heard them talking, though not what was said. It was too crowded in there, so she stayed out. Better to have the real docs checking out their patient while she...what? What should she do now that the immediate danger had passed?

She sat down on the rock they'd used to make their paltry meals, and as soon as she did, her body relaxed and she...sobbed. All of the fear and worry and stress and responsibility exited from her in the form of water and guttural sounds.

She'd kept things together for so long and it felt so good to put them down, finally. When she'd calmed, she realized the sun had crept up over the range, painting the sky a vibrant pink that blended into orange. A thin layer of low clouds that wove between the valleys took on the hues and deepened them. It gave the sky an ethereal glow.

We'll be okay. For the first time since they'd crashed, she genuinely believed it.

The four men all came out of the tent and stripped off their gloves. Their rescue team brought so many more supplies, she realized. What a damn gift—one she didn't ever think she'd be able to repay.

"Are you okay?" Reese asked, coming to her side and rubbing the base of her neck. She nodded, though she couldn't be sure it was true. Now that her most primal emotions were being processed, a myriad of others also popped up. With the emotions came questions.

What happened to her and Reese when they made it back to civilization?

Was her father okay?

How would she look Reese in the eyes and not lose her cool if he didn't agree now that the proposal for the clinic was absolutely necessary?

"Who did a chest tube in the field?" Greg asked, interrupting her thoughts. Erin was still recovering from the shock of finding not one rescuer, but three, and all of them physicians and best friends or brothers. It felt as if she was watching the scene from above.

The gift suddenly felt at risk.

Greg looked to Reese, who pointed to her. Heat rose to her cheeks. Of course, he'd assume the man in the group had performed the procedure.

"Um, me." She raised her hand like she was in class. "Reese's hand was injured so I took lead."

"You're also a surgeon?" he asked.

She shook her head. "No. I'm an emergency medical technician, but I've taken my Wilderness First Responder and had training on field medicine."

He regarded her warily.

Shit. Should she have let Reese take the credit for it? That didn't seem fair—not because she wanted the credit, but because she didn't want him to be blamed when something like this happened and she discovered she'd messed something up.

"You should consider going to med school and pursuing cardiothoracic surgery. Best chest tube I've seen out of my OR. You're a natural."

"Thanks," she said. Reese shot her a smile and mouthed, *Told ya.* She frowned. That might have been a dream at one point, but not for some time.

"And you used your hydration hose? Brilliant. Good job, Erin. Talk to me if you ever want to go that route—I know a shit ton of people in pretty influential places."

"He does," the other brother—Ian?—said. "And he never lets us forget it." He playfully slapped his brother on the shoulder as they cleaned up the wound, disinfected it with their fresh supplies, and redressed it. She watched on in awe as they worked seamlessly. How amazing would it be to work with a team like that? The kind of impact they could make…

It made it all the more imperative that the clinic get up and running. It would save lives and maybe bring in docs like these guys.

Erin was on a high she hadn't had experienced in years. It was amazing to watch docs that understood the elements and could manipulate them to their design. She might not be able to take on med school, but it was nice they thought she could.

I mean, how would I manage that with my dad? It wasn't possible, but that didn't mean it didn't have her thinking of ways it might be.

In three minutes, they had a makeshift stretcher made from tent poles. In ten more, they had Hector rigged up in a way that minimized movement around his open wounds.

"Looks good," Ethan said. "I'm five out from being cleaned up if you guys wanna check the site for anything that needs to come."

"We can leave what isn't necessary and come back for it," Erin agreed. In the end, they decided to leave the tents and just bring the sleeping bags so they could bed down if they didn't make it to the road to meet an ambulance before dark.

"Can I ask how you three fairy godfathers found us? This seems too good to be true, and I'm not entirely sure it actually happened. I mean, what are the chances three *surgeons* found us?" Reese asked. He chuckled, but Erin was curious about the same thing.

"Damned good luck," Ian said. "We take a trip each year to someplace remote—far enough our on-call service can't reach us, and this year, we voted on the Andes."

"But these aren't the—" Erin said.

"Exactly," Greg interrupted. "Because we weren't ready for the Andes, and these two thought we were. So I told them I wasn't going if they went ahead with it."

Ethan patted him on the back, then began rolling a sleeping bag. "Yeah, in all fairness, we were probably overshooting it. Either way, we threw a dart at three other choices across the country and landed here. Dumb luck."

"Dumb luck," Erin repeated, whispering it to herself. She and Reese—and Hector, too—owed these men more than they realized. And it all came down to a choice made long before they'd crashed. How wild life could be sometimes.

Like how wild you met a man like Reese to challenge you and invite you into the world of medicine again?

Maybe that, too. She didn't know what to do about Reese yet.

Greg and Ian packed up the medical supplies and made sure they were accessible, then Ian and Ethan took the first round with the stretcher. They made small talk for a bit, the brothers and friend sharing stories of some of their earlier exploits in other remote parts of the US and abroad.

They'd done some amazing travels and experienced some pretty close calls. Having three doctors on hand seemed to curb any emergent issues, they all agreed, though they'd been called upon to use their skill sets on more than one occasion.

"More like one per trip," Greg said. He didn't look pleased about that, but the other guys just laughed it off, so Erin didn't push. She had to admit, it felt so good to be moving again, even if she'd miss the makeshift outpost she and Reese had made.

And the connection they'd built.

Maybe it'll stay. No, that was naive, wishful thinking, and she couldn't afford anything as expensive as blind optimism. She lived in Hoodsport and Reese lived in Seattle. She had her dad to care for and he had a daughter. Their lives were just too different, even if they could each forgive the other their differences of opinion about life and its inherent risks.

Still, she slid up next to him on the path and hooked a pinkie in his. He gave her a weak smile.

"Are you okay?" she asked. He nodded, though the crease between his eyes said otherwise. "These guys are good. We'll be okay," she assured him. She wrapped her hand in his and squeezed. He squeezed back and then pulled her to a stop.

"Will we?" He searched her eyes and she knew he wasn't asking about the trek off the mountain. "Don't get me wrong—I'm so damned happy we're leaving, but… I'm worried everything will change when we get down."

"I know," she answered honestly. "We need to keep going right now, but I promise I'll talk to you about this tonight," she said.

Reese opened his mouth as if he wanted to say something else, but in the end, he closed it and shook his head, finally bringing her hand to his lips. He kissed her knuckles and smiled, but it still didn't reach his eyes.

Did he want to really give this a go? What would that look like?

"So I agree with Greg. You did a helluva job with that surgery," Ian said. She waited for him to add "for an EMT," but he didn't. "Any thoughts on where you'd go if you decided to leave Hoodsport?" he asked. "We could use someone like you in the surgical program in Manhattan."

"That's super generous of you to offer, but I've been trying to get an outpost clinic in Hoodsport so we can prevent situations like this from happening. That's why Dr. Vallen is here—he's sussing out the program. To be honest, that means more to me than school."

She didn't miss the look the doctors shared between them. Only Ethan shook his head, but the other two were grinning as if they'd won a prize. Reese was watching her with an unreadable expression on his face.

"Tell us more about that," Ian said, switching out with Greg for a spell. "We've been talking about what it would mean to build a program like that in the Appalachian Range, where the Appalachian Trail passes through. We have so many hikers that get injured and can't be flown out to a major hospital. A satellite program would be incredible."

"Why haven't you done that already?" she asked.

Ethan shrugged. "Only one of us lives in New York, and if we relocate, we want it to be somewhere we all want to be. None of us have ever agreed. If we did, we'd need someone like you who's done the legwork to talk us through it. Would you be interested in consulting?"

"It sounds amazing, but I guess it depends on Dr. Vallen's assessment of this program. My life is here, my community is here, but I know if we can't get this off the ground… I can't stay."

She didn't add her personal reasons for this project. Her father needed consistent care and shuttling to weekly treatments in order to keep his way of life and build him back to health. This was the only way to get him that. Without it, he'd need to be relocated as well, and the only way he'd ever consider it was if he could go someplace with the hope of the kind of life and adventure he had in Hoodsport when he was better.

When they got to a ridge where they had a clear line of sight of what looked like a road below, there was a beep from one of the backpacks.

"Sweet. Who needs to make a call? That was my cell letting me know we're back in service."

She needed to contact Lila immediately. She hesitated, though.

"Erin does," Reese said.

"Thank you," she said, hugging him. She knew how worried he was about Libby as well. Even a five-minute delay in hearing her voice was a lot. "I'll be quick."

"Call your dad, too," he said.

She squeezed him tighter and tried not to notice

how good it felt to have her arms around him again. Sure, they were in the middle of a rescue after a week in the wilderness, but…she missed him.

Erin called Lila, who wept, but then gone serious and told her not to worry—everything was fine there. She got her dad on the line next, only to find out he'd been shacking up with his neighbor, Julie, while Erin was gone. He'd been, in his words, "worried, sure. But I knew you were gonna be fine. I taught you all about how to survive out there in the winter, so it was just a matter of when you came home, not if." He'd gone to the hospital and decided he'd probably just stay with Julie for a bit, either way. Apparently, he'd finally realized there was something brewing between them and "she was a lot of fun."

She appreciated her father's confidence; however, it would have been nice if someone was there, worried about her. A weariness settled over her, only partially because of the ordeal they'd just endured.

She'd been carrying the weight of everything, of everyone in her life. She thought back to Reese's question about wanting to go back to medical school. His saying that it was time she did something for herself, finally.

On paper, it sounded like a great idea, but life—and everything happening in it of late—was too heavy, and something had to be put down. But what? Her dad was being cared for—at least in theory—by a neighbor ten years his junior. They'd been flirting for years, and must have taken the leap to more than friends while she was…away. Was Julie aware of his medical needs, or was she just enjoying playing house? Could Erin put *that* down long enough to finally, twenty-five years later, make a life for herself? She wasn't sure.

All she knew was that, in theory, she was happy for her dad. Just not what it meant for her… Her whole life had been dedicated to the man.

Reese tapped her, and she opened her eyes to the guys in lighthearted conversation.

"If you don't keep her," Ian said, his tone light and jovial, "we're gonna steal her."

Erin glanced at Reese, and when he met her gaze, it wasn't what she'd expected. His eyes were dark, his eyebrows pulled tight and serious. The opposite of how they'd been each of the past few nights.

"What do you mean?" she asked.

"We want to steal you for our own project if Dr. Vallen here doesn't take yours and run with it."

Reese shrugged. "Money's tight with the board—it's anyone's guess. If you have something better to offer, Erin should take it."

What?! she wanted to scream. *You want me to take something other than the one thing I've spent literal years building?!*

Then another realization, this one damning.

He isn't going to help me green-light the project. Sleeping with her must have been some sort of consolation prize, and it was with that light-bulb moment that she recognized the same thing she'd known since she was eight years old.

She could only count on herself when it came to building a life she wanted, and it was past time she stopped hoping for more. Reese Vallen was just like everyone else in her life.

He'd leave as soon as he could, and like the rest of the people she'd known, she'd learn to live without him, too.

CHAPTER TEN

THEY MADE IT off the mountain and an ambulance met them at the Belfair clinic. It would still be a drive to Seattle Memorial, but they were safe. Reese couldn't feel anything about that, though. Not relief, not exhaustion—nothing. Partly because he was worried about Hector and what they'd discover about his healing, or lack of it. But also because he'd been confused about Erin's shift on how she treated him when the guys were around.

Mostly, he was still in shock that any of this had happened, and that, after a week of wondering whether any of them would survive, they were back, passing fast-food restaurants and people on the patios of pubs in the afternoon sun as if their whole world hadn't ended.

It was so surreal.

Hector was immediately put on IV antibiotics. He was also given a slew of tests to see how his blood was handling the clotting concern. The team said they'd fill in the docs as soon as they knew anything.

Erin and Reese were both taken to exam rooms

at the same time to be cleared by a team, and ended up back in the waiting room within moments of one another.

"You're okay?" he asked. He held his breath until she nodded.

"Yep. You?"

He nodded as well. "Bumps and bruises, but nothing I can't heal from with a little rest."

"Same."

There was a pause as both of them considered what rest might be like. He wondered if she was thinking—as he was—that she'd like them to take some time together, to explore whatever they'd built in the mountains.

The hospital offered him and Erin a flight back, but both of them emphatically shouted, "No!" at the same time.

"Lila can probably come get me and bring your things with her," Erin offered. So she wasn't thinking the same thing at all. She was shoving him off like the past week hadn't happened. His heart lurched, even though he should have been glad he got to go home, to put the whole mess behind them.

"That's okay. I'll rent a car and drive us back," he told her. They'd decided to wait to meet Hector's wife, who was being brought in by a friend the long way around and was still an hour out. "Then I can take it back when I head home. I still have some, um, final reporting to do out there." That wasn't entirely true, but he wasn't ready to say goodbye to her just yet, even if he couldn't figure out what that meant.

"How did you get to Hoodsport originally? Didn't you drive?"

He shook his head. "I was dropped off by the head of my team, who was on her way to the coast with her wife. By now, they're probably back in Seattle."

"Oh. This works, then."

He nodded.

The air was still tense between them. He needed to run the numbers and get them to his board in Seattle, but he wished he could just tell them the pathos-filled version. They needed the clinic, and him almost losing his life proved that exponentially.

Hector's wife came in and gave them both long hugs and tears of gratitude for keeping her husband alive. Then, she prayed they wouldn't think she was rude, but she just wanted to go be with Hector. Both Erin and Reese agreed that was the only place she should be and told her they'd check in with her the next day to find out how Hector was doing. The only caveat they gave was if something happened that night; then, they wanted to know so they could come support her, though everyone agreed they hoped not to see each other until the next day.

Reese slipped away to call his mom.

She answered and broke into sobs.

"I thought—" she choked out. He was nodding even though she couldn't see him.

"I know. Me, too. I'm so sorry. I would have said

something that first day, but I didn't want you to worry, not after..." He and his mom hadn't ever talked about Allie, not really. Maybe it was time they did. "After Allie's death."

She sniffled and his heart ached. "I'm just glad you're okay. But now that you are, I need to talk to you. It can't wait anymore."

He watched the patients come in and out of the hospital, worry settling deep in his chest.

"What's wrong, Mom?"

"Nothing. You're home and safe. But you're also a fraction of the man you used to be. What happened to Allie that day was her own fault, and I've seen the way it crippled you from chasing your own dreams. I don't like sitting in worry wondering if you've survived a helicopter crash, but I also don't like watching you waste your life away."

He let that simmer. She was right; he'd felt the same while he and Erin were in the mountains. They'd been facing death, but he'd never felt so alive.

"I want to tackle that with you, but before that, in the spirit of what you've said, can I ask a favor?" She said yes, of course, he could. He wanted to see if he could have a day or two to get his emotions in check and then come to them. He missed his daughter something fierce, but she still didn't know what had happened to him, and if he saw her now, he'd break down.

He needed a minute to get himself right before he scared her with his big feelings. She'd already lost a mother—to be the dad she deserved, he needed a breath.

His mom agreed it was the best decision for all of them and swore she loved the time with her granddaughter, who, she further assured him, was being spoiled rotten and wasn't worried at all about when he'd come home—just that he would.

"I love you," he told her. Another thing they often neglected to say. Not anymore.

"I love you, too, Reese. So much."

His heart was lighter after having talked to her. At first. Then, a heavy weight settled into the space previously occupied by worry about his mother and daughter.

Erin. He liked her…maybe even felt something more than that. But what could come of it? Here, in his home, he knew… Their worlds were too different.

"Can I make a suggestion?" he asked when he got back to her. He wanted the time he was sorting through his emotions to be put to good use for Erin's project. It was necessary, that was for sure, and it was the least he could do. They'd made it through the risky rescue, but it had only shone a light on what was really at risk—his heart and his daughter's stability. He needed to protect both, and the only way he could do that was to put distance between him and where he felt his energy being pulled.

"Sure," she said.

"Let's get an emergency board meeting on the

books and show them your proposal while we give our testimony from the crash and rescues we've been a part of the past week. There's no way they won't fund it with my approval and our harrowing experience."

"You want to tell the board they should support my proposal for the clinic? That they should build a clinic in rural western Washington, not…somewhere else?"

"Of course, I want to keep you—and the clinic—in rural Washington. Where else would it be? I thought I'd been pretty clear how I felt…about the project," he added, for clarity. "But maybe not?"

"No, I mean, I heard you, but… I guess I assumed it was just for show."

His confusion knew no bounds. "To be honest, in the beginning, I was struggling to see the need for such expenditure outside the county. But with the clinic, we wouldn't have needed to fly to Seattle with the hiker and we would've been spared this whole week. Why would you think I would have lied to you this whole time?" he asked her.

"Because you told the 'Fabulous Three,'" she said, quoting the nickname he'd unofficially given the three docs, "if they had something better to offer, they should."

It all made sense now. She'd heard that as a lack of support. He didn't see a way for them to be together, not in the way they were in the mountains, anyway. But he cared for her, supported her vision.

You want her, too, don't you? His heart wasn't

completely off base, but he worried he'd need to follow his head on this one.

People funneled in and out of the waiting room and Reese fought the urge to ask them what they needed. He couldn't be a help to anyone else until he'd taken care of himself…and his daughter, too.

"Erin, I want you happy. If the board doesn't give you the answer you're looking for, I wanted you to have options." The way she was looking at him, with wide, questioning eyes, had him worried, so he rolled his statement over in his head. "I mean, you're the best doctor I've ever worked with regardless of a degree, so thanks."

He hated that, without being clear about the way he felt—which he'd do, soon—he'd hedged and made their connection solely about work. Sure, she was a damn fine doctor—or EMT, officially. But she was also someone he loved spending time with. Maybe they could stay friends. He could see bringing his daughter out to the mountains to play and meet up with Erin…

Yeah, like a sweet little family. After sleeping together and falling for one another in the mountains. That won't be confusing for anyone.

Ugh. He wished it was simpler. That she lived closer or was willing to move. Because as he mulled it over, the truth was, he was curious about her, but he needed to figure out what he wanted to do now that…something had shifted in him. How to be there for his daughter. He couldn't uproot her to follow a crush, could he?

He should address those feelings—hell, wasn't that what he'd taken this time away from Libby for?

Instead, he hedged again.

"Hey, why'd you call me 'Dr. Vallen' when we were with the other docs?" he asked. Not that this line of questioning was any better. His ability to keep his mouth shut around her until he could phrase things properly was just as bad as it'd been since they met. Oof.

She frowned.

"Because we were talking about medicine. It seemed appropriate. You aren't jealous, are you?" she asked. His chest roared with heat at her use of a word he'd kept under lock and key. Not because the three docs were talented and skilled, or anything like that—Reese wasn't so naive to think that he didn't possess any of those qualities. He was damn good at what he did.

Is it because they're handsome and if you aren't going to pursue her, it means one of them can?

Hmm. He hadn't considered that. Nor was it helpful to now.

His jealousy—because, yes, he could name it now that she had—was about what they could offer her that he couldn't. She had the clinic and maybe medical school to look forward to. Seattle Memorial was a teaching hospital, and the University of Washington did have a well-regarded medical school program. But how could he ask her to give up what she had in Hoodsport to consider moving to a city—moreover, one for him, and not the career she was chasing? Especially because he wasn't sure what he could offer her.

"I am, actually." She looked as shocked as he felt about the admission. "I mean, they have everything you're looking for—in a team for your clinic, I mean." It was likely they could offer her more outside of work as well, seeing as how they all shared her interests and were far more naturally adventurous than Reese was.

There was that unhelpful line of thinking again…

"You…*what*?" she asked. "I mean… But, *why*?" He shrugged. "Professionally or…something else?" she asked.

The guys who'd rescued them had the benefit of not knowing her the way he'd come to the past week, which meant they could give her the world with no strings attached. They also seemed to know what they were doing and wanted her for a project that seemed infinitely bigger than the one she'd proposed. Maybe they were a better fit.

But he wasn't willing to give her up entirely, either, not yet. They might not have a future, but they did work so damn well together.

Finally. Jeez.

And, no, not just in a professional capacity, either. This clinic mattered to her, and she mattered to him—it was useless to deny that.

He wanted her, as his heart had suggested. He didn't know what that would mean, since there were a lot of semantics to figure out, but maybe the universe would conspire to help them out like it had when it'd sent the docs to their rescue in the first place.

If not, they'd always have the memories.

As if that's enough for you...

"Erin," he said, unsure what he'd follow that with. "I like you, and I think you're brilliant. I don't know what that means since I'm in Seattle permanently, but I don't want to leave you yet." Well, that was one way of making space between them. Good grief, he couldn't trust himself, could he?

She laughed and glanced around, as if realizing they were having a very private conversation in a very public place.

"Would you like to talk about this somewhere less...public?" he asked.

"Sure. Yeah. But, what about your daughter? Does she need you?"

He didn't want this woman out of his sight tonight, which gave him an idea. Maybe they could extend their uncertain future while he took care of himself before his reunion with his daughter.

"Nope. I asked my mom to take care of her a day or two more so I don't lose my mind when I see her. I haven't had a real meal, real sleep, or real safety in a week. If I get ahold of her, I'm afraid I'll break down and scare her. I'd rather take a couple minutes to get my head on right. Would you—" He didn't know how to ask her to stay with him without sounding like a horny jerk. Especially given that he couldn't offer her anything. "I'm heading home alone for two nights, and if you'd like and don't have to be back right away, we could pitch to the board and otherwise order takeout from the best restaurants in Seattle, and sleep in and…"

He was rambling. *See? This is what happens when you don't have a plan.*

"I mean, you don't have to come by and I can take you back inst—"

Erin leaned over the seat and kissed him on the cheek. The spot beneath her lips was hot with the memory of shared desire in the tent each night. She was going to be impossible to leave behind, wasn't she? Worse, if he had memories of her in his city. But the fact remained—she'd never want to live in the city, and he and his daughter were established there.

This could be fun and beautiful, but it was also temporary. Hopefully, a friendship would blossom where passion had planted the seeds. Because he also couldn't imagine ever saying goodbye forever to her.

What if she doesn't want the in-between like you do?

He'd cross that bridge then.

"I want to."

He was irrationally happy to hear that. In fact, if he was being honest with himself, he was hoping she'd stay when he asked his mom for time. Not only because he liked her—which he did—but also because he felt like the healing he needed to do was only possible with her by his side. He couldn't say why, just that it's what he believed. That Libby wouldn't be there added some level of safety. The one holdup he had was them meeting before he and Erin had time to figure out what they were. Once they did…he couldn't stop picturing what possibilities might happen then. But he couldn't get ahead of himself.

"I think your suggestion about healing before we go back to real life is a good one. Or maybe not fully healing or we might not ever go back."

She laughed, but had no idea how right she was. He'd seen patients and their families undergo similar traumas, and they were always different on the other side. It would be the same for him and Erin, the permanent shift in perspective, but…

Maybe that was a good thing. He'd been hiding for some time and it took nearly dying to really feel alive again.

Who knew?

Only Erin and all the people like her.

Touché.

All he knew was that he'd almost lost her and he didn't want that to happen ever again. Not when he'd just found her—the first person to make him even think about risking his heart again. It may not be that he had a lot to offer her from an emotional standpoint, but this was a start, at least.

"Then let's get out of here," he said.

"Lead the way."

He'd never been more ready to meet a request in his life.

* * *

They got to his house and showered separately. Erin went first and took nearly ten minutes in the hot water. He was so grateful she had the time to clean up and relax, but it was torture to imagine the body he'd grown used to naked and wet, and just beyond the closed door. For a week, they'd been together as they'd kept Hector alive, ate, slept, almost every minute except when she'd bathe at the creek or go in search of help.

Now, he craved that closeness again.

He showered much quicker, the desperation to lie with her, to just relax with her in his arms, an all-consuming desire at this point. Not exactly a safe path to an exit strategy, as he'd hoped.

When they were both in his bedroom, he felt like he could finally exhale.

"Come here," he said, pulling her into an embrace on the bed. He tucked her against his shoulder. He'd thought about it in the shower. He wanted to use the time to let her know how he felt about her, aside from the medicine, the trauma, the distance metaphorically and physically between their lives. To see what she thought about them, about her place in Hoodsport. "I have something to tell you."

She nuzzled against him, the soft give of the mattress beneath them a new concept. It was unfamiliar, but not unwelcome.

"What's that?" she asked. Her hand rested easily on his chest, as if worried that pushing too much would scare him off. He knew where her fear originated from, but not how to calm it. All he could do was hold her, let her know that he might not be able to pick up his life and move to western Washington, but he wasn't going anywhere, either. He could be there for her no matter where his life was, in some capacity, anyway.

At least, that was his hope.

"Before I get to that, have you realized how—"

"How absolutely spectacular it is to lie on a real mattress?"

He laughed.

"That's exactly what I was going to say. It's so weird to be… Back. You know?"

She nodded against his chest, a gesture he was familiar with from their time in the mountains. How he'd ever forget it—or her—was beyond him. He was different from that first hike he'd shared with her; spending almost a week lost in the wilderness and keeping a man alive while falling for a woman he was diametrically opposed to had irrevocably altered his DNA.

"I do. When I got in the shower, I actually braced for the cold, when I should have been preparing my skin for how scorching hot it would feel after bathing in the creek all week. I like these creature comforts, but can I share something?"

He nodded this time, though he knew she couldn't feel or see it.

"You miss it?" he asked.

She gazed up at him. "I do."

He kissed the top of her head and had to say, he preferred the natural scent she'd had when she'd come back from the creek, her cold and wet hair fresh instead of plied with product the hotels gave out. Who'd have thought the city doctor would find more than just peace in the outdoors?

"Me, too," he admitted. Something shifted in his chest. The things he'd thought were important still were, but so was something else…

"Weird, isn't it?" She leaned up and met his gaze. It *was* weird, but that wasn't the weirdest part about all of what had occurred. Nor was finding the shared need for the program she'd pitched. No, the strangest thing was realizing that he'd thought he was coming around to discovering he actually liked the outdoors, even with the risk it presented, but that was only half the story.

He had fallen in love with the mountains through Erin's eyes and how she saw them.

He was falling in love with Erin.

There wasn't any big mental fireworks that went off in his head, no aha moment in his heart at the realization. Just a settling of pieces that had been floating around in his chest as they found a home, as if the answer had been there all along.

Hmm.

It didn't change his need to figure stuff out for his daughter, for himself, but it was there, the hint of something more than there'd been before.

"Anyway, what did you want to tell me?" she asked.

Well, that was a loaded question. He still wanted to "tell" her the same thing as before, but the motivations behind it were different than they'd been moments ago.

He tilted her chin up and kissed her, and found something he appreciated about being back in civilization. With proper care and hydration, Erin's lips were the softest damn thing… They made the comforter feel like a stiff board.

"Mmm," she moaned into his lips. "I like this conversation."

He nipped at her earlobe with his teeth, eliciting a squeal of delight. Hell, he loved that sound.

"Then you're really gonna love what comes next."

His hands slipped under her nightshirt and cupped her breasts. She arched her back and he took the opportunity to kiss her neck, trail his tongue along her collarbone, then lean into her until he could reach her nipples. He sucked on them until they hardened for him, meaning he could flick them with his tongue, a guaranteed way to make her—

"Oh, my… Yes, please," she purred. There it was.

She slipped her panties off and his finger found her wet and ready for him.

"Tell me what you want," he whispered in her ear. She shivered and grinned up at him.

"Mmm-hmm. You told me you had something to say to me, so say it." His eyebrows rose in both invitation and question. She only nodded. "I want to hear anything you need to tell me."

It was his turn to smile, and for a split second, before he dived into her folds with his tongue to start the "conversation" there, he wondered how he'd gotten so lucky. He had an amazing, brave, brilliant woman in his arms and was about to spend the night loving her until they both had nothing left.

What more could he want? That question surprised him.

The answer was simple. *I want you.*

The next morning, a text from his mother awoke him. Erin was in the bathroom, brushing her teeth by the sounds of it.

I'm coming in with Libby to grab some school clothes. All clear?

No, it was decidedly not. He glanced around the room to see the detritus that resulted from a night of passionate lovemaking. Clothes and blankets and pillows and bedroom furniture were strewn in disarray. It turned out that when they had the run of an actual bedroom, they made damn good use of it.

"Hey, Erin?" he called out.

"Mmm?" she replied, coming out with the toothbrush in her mouth. God, she was adorable.

"My mom is on the way with Libby. Do you want to meet her?"

She stopped brushing her teeth. The look in her

eyes reminded him of when they'd spent the first night together in the tent. She'd awoken, and gazed at him the same way, as if it could convey a question.

He'd discovered what the look was that morning—was he okay with what they'd done? Was the question the same now?

"I'd love for you two to meet, if that makes a difference. You two are similar enough I'll probably regret that, but—" He laughed. "But I think it would be…nice to see how you two get on."

She didn't say anything, so he added, "I don't want to add to your stress, but it's what I pictured up there, wondering how you two would get along. I just wanted to be sure you wanted it, too, that you and I were on the same page."

It might illuminate if he and Erin might have more than just the proposal between them. He still couldn't see what that might be, but knowing how his daughter and Erin got along at least gave him hope.

"Mmm, 'kay," she whispered, and some toothpaste slipped past her lip. "No stress." She smiled and ran back to the bathroom.

He texted his mother back.

Not yet, but it's fine. Erin can meet Libby. It was the first step in seeing if and how Erin would want to be in his life. Parenting was his first priority, over medicine. It sounded as if she understood, since caring for her father, though different, was of the utmost importance to her. Thanks, Mom. I appreciate your help while we navigate this return to real life.

No problem. We had a great time together, but she wants a specific dress. And, hon, I know I said it a lot, but I'm just eternally grateful you three are okay.

They were, too. Or would be. Hector had a long road to go as he healed, but he'd get to see his kid be born, so that had to count for something.

Was it real life for him and Erin, though? Sure, they got to defend the proposal and hopefully get preliminary funding for her project, thanks to the help of the three docs they'd met on the trail—doctors they owed more than a small debt of gratitude to for rescuing them, too. But other than that, they'd been bedded down and "resting" and needed to figure out what came next for both of them.

"I'm gonna shower since my mom is bringing Libby by. Want to join?" he asked.

Panic widened her eyes. "They're coming right now?"

He kissed her deeply and pulled her by her hand back toward the bathroom. "It's fine. We have time to clean up."

The look on Erin's face was unreadable, but she nodded, her bottom lip pulled between her teeth. He would count that as an enthusiastic yes.

When the water was on and warm, he got to work cleaning Erin's body, top to bottom, but first made sure to finish what they'd started the night before, getting them dirtier in the process.

He didn't think he'd ever get sick of loving this woman's body against his. They were magnets, drawn not just to each other, but that pulled more out of the other. It was a rare kind of alchemy, that was for sure.

But was it enough?

Reese went back and forth when he got out of the shower and went in search of real clothes for the first time in over a week.

Two options stood in front of him. The one he was facing at the moment, the one his nights with Erin demanded he walk closer to with each kiss, each embrace, each whisper of love, was perched on a cliffside. Sure, the view was spectacular, but one wrong move and he wouldn't just slide down the embankment; he was so high up, he'd fall off the edge to his death.

The other option—the one here in Seattle with the hospital, doing what he'd been doing when he met Erin—positioned him on safe, stable ground that was flat and posed little-to-no risks. At least on the outside.

He rolled through the report again, his mind seeing actual faces instead of the numbers on the page. Hector's relief when he was brought into Seattle. The climber's bloodstained cheeks smiling through the pain when they made it to medical help. Erin's contented sigh as she handed over care of her patients and knew she'd done her best.

He'd done the right thing in supporting her project, that much he knew. But that was for the program, the community, the medicine.

If he really was falling for Erin, which he was pretty damn sure he was, what was he prepared to do for *her*? To support *her*?

An idea came to him, but he needed to be certain it was the right move and that all the pieces would fit if he went for it.

The great outdoors presented the same amount of risk as it always had. The difference was, he knew how to mitigate those dangers, and how to fix some of the consequences that came with playing in an unknown environment.

But this was different—love was the greatest risk of all, because it couldn't be mitigated, controlled, or manipulated. And the consequences were dire.

If it failed, he'd be taking them both off the cliff and he wasn't sure either would survive the fall.

CHAPTER ELEVEN

ERIN TURNED THE stuffed animal over in her hands.

"So this is an axolotl?" she asked the young girl. Libby nodded, her tiny curls bouncing with the gesture. "It's so cute."

"Her name is Lotty and she lives in Mexico. I want to go to Mexico, but Daddy said it's too dangerous. I don't care, though."

Erin stifled a giggle. Libby was only going to grow more interested in travel if she was prevented from doing it. She knew that firsthand.

"She doesn't have a mother, either," Libby added.

Erin noted the thump of her heart at those words. It picked up pace and felt as if it slammed against her rib cage.

"How do you know that?" Erin asked. Her throat felt dry, scratchy, and heat built behind her eyes.

"Because lotsa animals don't have mothers. The eggs raise themselves, Daddy says."

Erin knew what Libby was talking about. When she was smaller—not quite as young as Libby, but close—she'd gone to her library and asked the librarian the one question she was afraid of asking her father. *Did everyone have a mother except her?* The librarian had been kind and shown her all the animals that fended for themselves after birth. Axolotls were one of them.

"That's true," she said. She tried on a smile and tucked the blanket around the girl and her stuffed animal. It was late, but at least they could sleep in the next morning since Libby would be going to her grandmother's. "She's lucky to have you."

Libby beamed and Erin couldn't help the wave of affection she had for the girl. Yes, they were similar, as Reese had shared. But not just because they'd been raised motherless. The girl was inquisitive, happy, and had a sense of adventure her dad didn't share.

"Do you have a mother?"

Erin froze. Reese had gone to get Libby a glass of water. What was taking him so long?

"Um, no. I mean, like you, I had one at first, but also like you, I was raised by my father."

Libby's eyebrows furrowed and she nodded.

"Will you be like a mom if you stay here with me?"

Reese's throat cleared behind them. He met Erin's gaze. She bit her bottom lip. That question was on her mind as well, and no doubt was on Reese's to some degree.

"I've got your water, hon, but I have to warn you, the dinosaur on this one is missing a leg. Must've lost it in the battle with the dishwasher."

Libby gasped, her inquisition around motherhood forgotten as she looked at the dinosaur sticker that had, indeed, lost a leg.

"Oh, Betsy. I'll fix it tomorrow," Libby said. Erin smiled and left the father and daughter to finish their bedtime routine. The thing was, the moment she'd met the young girl, she had fallen for her as much as she had the girl's father. But something about the last question she'd asked gave her pause.

What if she got close to Libby and she and Reese broke up? Then Libby would be forced through another abandonment. At least, that was how it would seem...

She settled on the couch.

A still quiet blanketed the house after a few minutes. Erin held a glass of wine in her hands and it tasted like...heaven. The whole place she was in at that moment was heaven, actually. She'd been shacked up with Reese for a week now, and every day she spent here made it harder to want to go home.

And she had to go home, eventually, anyway.

It wasn't just that his house in Seattle overlooked the Puget Sound and she could see and hear the ships coming in, she could watch the ferry boats transporting Bainbridge residents into the city, and she could see Mount Rainier from the big bay window in the master suite. It wasn't just the magnificent food—each meal from a different culture she'd always wanted to try but couldn't access in her small rural..."town." "Village" was more like it. It also wasn't the nightly walk they took as a small family through the Craftsman homes in the Queen Anne neighborhood, the Space Needle as their guide. It wasn't the feeling of peace Erin felt, a calm she had struggled to re-create in her adult life, having missed it most of her childhood.

That was all wonderful, but all of it was secondary to how comfortable she felt with Reese. None of the rest mattered like he and his daughter did. Putting Libby to bed or talking to her about animals at the zoo, and which ones might want to be friends if they met in the wild, was the highlight of her year. Worse was Reese. When she hugged him, she knew she'd found home in a person and that scared the crap out of her.

"She's asleep, finally," he said, coming into the room and grabbing the wine from her hands and taking a sip. "Mmm. I take it back, I'm going to have a glass, too."

"Told you so." She winked and stole her glass back from him, laughing as he tried to hold on to it. "No way. Get your own."

He took her in an embrace.

"What if I like yours because it's had your lips on it?" he whispered. She shivered at the flirtation and warmth from his breath on her neck. The heat pressed south, and moisture pooled in her panties. Good grief, this man knew just the way to her pleasure without even touching her. It was both beautiful and disorienting, like being lost in a different kind of wilderness.

"Can I ask you a serious question?" she asked.

She'd kept her inquiries light the past week, not wanting to disrupt the still waters that were healing them from their most immediate trauma. However, turbulent seas lay beneath the surface from long before they'd met. And the feeling of home meant nothing if they couldn't face the stormy weather together.

Do you want that? To let him in enough to go through this together?

She didn't know, but she knew she liked him enough to try and see. That was big for her. It was enough, at least for now.

"Of course. I think we've earned that at least," he teased, kissing her.

"I know she left you both, but would you tell me what happened with Libby's mom? Libby seems pretty self-aware for as young as she is. Did she know her mom at all?"

Reese took Erin's wine and this time she let him. He sipped it, then put the glass on the table so he could take her hands in his. He sighed, but if she didn't know any better, it seemed like…relief.

"She didn't. Jack-Lynn, my ex-wife, wanted to be free and clear of us both. Or, at least, she did at the end. I think we were too much of an encumbrance to the life she wanted to live."

Erin couldn't imagine walking away from her daughter and husband—but Reese's story wasn't unique. Erin had lived it from Libby's perspective and it hadn't helped her understanding of the kind of woman who'd leave at all.

"But she chose you, chose to have a baby. Why would she leave?"

"That's the million-dollar question, but I've had enough therapy I know I wasn't helpful when I lost my sister. I became afraid of my own shadow for a while and Jack-Lynn was made of nothing but adventure and optimism. She couldn't understand or empathize with my sadness and grief. Nor could she be patient as I worked my way back to the man I was before I lost Allie. She wasn't always like that," he said, answering a question that had been on the tip of Erin's tongue since the start of this conversation.

Erin squeezed his hands, so much more aware of the man she'd met at the outpost that day. He'd been scared and closed off, but now she could see why. And through to the kind of fear he'd had to overcome to be there for her in those terrifying moments when she'd been hopeless and fearful herself.

"I'm so sorry. For you and Libby."

He tightened his grip on her hands at that last comment.

"Thanks. And thanks for asking. It can't be easy to talk about, given what you've been through, either."

She shrugged. "It isn't, but on some level I understand my mom all these years later—or at least the way life can pigeonhole us. I am pretty tied to the life I live, if for no other reason than my dad's health. As much as I want to some days, despite loving what I do in Hoodsport, I can't leave. That must have been stifling for her. For all of them."

Reese worried his bottom lip as if he wanted to ask something, say something more.

"You mean your ex?"

She'd never really talked about that with anyone, not even Lila. She nodded. Reese drew all kinds of truths out of her—part of why she was so comfortable, and also why it scared her to death.

"He was the same as the rest of them. Life was too small there for him, so even though we were engaged, he couldn't wait for me to 'figure out' who meant more—him or my dad."

"What an ass." She nodded. "I can't imagine life being too small with you," Reese whispered, kissing the top of her hand. It was the nicest thing she'd ever heard, but what did it mean?

"I have another question," she said. "Totally different subject, though."

"Shoot. I'm good at this." Relief seemed to flood his features again at moving on from the last subject.

"Are you ready for tomorrow?" she asked him. They were meeting with the board to discuss the particulars of the clinic that had been green-lit. "Want to go over it in more detail?"

His grin was positively wicked.

"I want to go over something in extreme detail, but not our presentation."

He took her glass from her again, this time without hesitation from her. He put it on the coffee table and leaned her back on the couch. He placed a pillow under the small of her back, tilting her hips up.

She bit her bottom lip in anticipation.

He tugged at her silk pajama bottoms, a gift he'd brought her back from picking up Libby the first morning she'd returned to day care.

He ran a hand down her core before slipping a finger inside her. She knew what he'd find—she was more than wet and ready for him. She nodded. Their foreplay—kissing and touching and tasting—was glorious and so appreciated. But at that moment, she needed to be filled by this man.

"Take me," she said. He nodded and slipped out of his pants. "You are so beautiful," she murmured.

"I'm yours," he whispered back. At the same time, he entered her, and she cried out, grabbing a pillow to cover her scream. She'd had partners that knew what they were doing in the past, but no one had ever filled her so completely and brought her so much pleasure simultaneously.

It was hard to imagine going home because she really, truly, couldn't picture what life looked like without Reese in it.

He thrust inside her, erasing the intrusive thoughts and bringing her back to the now.

"Oh," she moaned. "You feel so damn good, Reese." His groan was matched by a deep thrust that rocked her to her core. "Yes, please. That," she breathed out on a satisfied sigh.

"Erin, I am not going to last two seconds if I

keep this up. You're so tight and perfect, it's undoing me."

"Come for me," she said, echoing something he'd told her when they'd been back in the tent. "I want you inside me when you come. I want to feel every last thrust as you let my body bring you there."

He growled a primal sound that brought her to the edge of her own orgasm. "You, too, love."

Her eyes widened and she couldn't stop the flood of desire that took her over the cliff at the same time Reese groaned and bucked inside her. He collapsed beside her as she panted, desperate for breath and for him to be closer—always closer.

"That was—" he said, minutes later when he was still shivering inside her embrace.

"It damn well was," she said, finishing for him. "I'm glad Libby sleeps soundly."

He laughed and lifted his head, even though they could see down the hallway and were in the clear.

He exhaled and lay on the pillow next to her shoulder, tracing her breasts and nipples until she felt another wave of want building.

"Why did that feel so damn different?" he asked. "Nothing's different with you, you know, down there, is it?"

She giggled. "No," she answered. "I'm not near my period, but I may be ovulating. That shouldn't make a difference, though." She appreciated that she could talk about her body with Reese since he was a physician and didn't shy away from topics about her. It was another thing that was refreshing about them.

The thing she couldn't say was her suspicion as to why it'd felt so different that time. Because he was right—it was so much more intense than any other time they'd come at the same time. It was her most intense orgasm ever, but she wasn't ready to voice that, either.

They'd had some spectacular sex, but this was the closest they'd come to sharing what was in their hearts, not just their bodies.

He'd called her "love" and told her he was all hers. She'd wanted to answer the thing on the tip of her tongue—that she was falling for him. But that was so far off-limits, she might as well have left the words on the top of the cliff and buried them there.

His phone rang, a welcome distraction from her feelings.

"This is Dr. Vallen." She flinched ever so slightly at the "Dr." in his greeting. It just rolled off his tongue so easily. Of course, it did; it was so earned. That didn't mean she wasn't a little bit jealous—just a little—that he could say it.

Maybe it was being back in the city, his home turf, that led to his confidence. Or perhaps it was due to his time in the Olympic Range that brought this side of him out, honed him into a competent, sexy doctor she wanted in every way she'd ever wanted a man.

To be his lover, sure. But his partner, his colleague, and his friend mattered even more.

He was so steady, she wondered why she'd ever questioned his authority. His strength, solid calm, and support were those of a born leader, not a man who would be intimidated by a small hike in the backcountry.

He sat up and scooted off the couch.

"Can I make you tea?" he whispered, throwing on his gray sweats. To the person on the other end, he said, "Okay. I understand, even if I don't agree. When?"

She shook her head. "No thanks," she whispered back. Who was on the phone? she wondered. It wasn't her business because she wasn't his girlfriend, his spouse, or his partner. What was she, then?

"I'm gonna finish my wine and go brush my teeth. I'm wiped and want to be ready for tomorrow. We haven't exactly been great at catching up with sleep since we got back," she teased. He smiled and walked out of the room.

Like they'd done on the mountain, they'd fallen into a routine in the city, too.

They would wake in one another's arms before the sun was even up, make love until they were both sated and sweaty, then shower. She'd work on the particulars of the clinic proposal—budgetary, mostly, like whom to hire, how much they would cost to retain, what the rooms should be outfitted with. Reese went into work, dropping Libby off on the way, then came back to her at lunch, where they'd make love again, dripping in one another's embrace until he was pulled back to the office for one meeting or another. Once, they'd broken their schedule and gone out to dinner, but otherwise, she and Reese cooked together, had a glass of wine, and he put Libby to bed while she watched the city below them.

It never slept, either. Which was fitting, since she and Reese made love late into the night, unable to sate their shared desire. It was like being weaned off a drug when she was away from him for even a couple hours. It wasn't healthy, but damn, did it feel too good to quit him.

"I'll be right back," he said. She nodded and leaned back against the cushion and pillow. She didn't need her wine—she needed to figure out what she was doing before this "thing" they'd started gained too much momentum and took off without her.

She'd been on a current, swept away by others' needs instead of paddling up her own stream at her own pace. This wasn't really any different, not without making a conscious choice about what to do and talking to him about the potential outcomes.

He came back, a frown on his face.

"What happened?" she asked. He sat on the edge of the couch as far as he could from her. He never wanted to be more than suffocatingly close to her. Worry crept into her heart where pure joy had pushed it out earlier. It nuzzled in close, sending a shiver up her spine.

She pulled the fleece blanket from the back of the couch over her.

"There was an investigation into Hector's care and it brought up some questions about the clinic proposal." The shiver grew until she couldn't control it. "They'd like us to come in and iron out some 'grave concerns,'" he added.

"What kind of concerns?"

He shook his head and ran a hand through his hair. The sigh he let out was one of pure exhaustion…and his own brand of worry. His eyes held the same caged look as the day he'd met her, which seemed like it was years ago, instead of weeks.

"Could they stop the proposal? I mean, you said tomorrow was a formality," she said when he didn't answer. Nor did he meet her gaze. What the actual hell had changed to dismantle everything they'd built in a matter of minutes?

"They heard from the docs who rescued us that you were the one to complete the procedure and they want to talk about your credentials to perform such a complicated surgery. They also want to know who will be running the clinic if cases like this come through in the future. Right now, without a doctor on-site, they can't green-light the clinic. That, and some other issues this creates, I guess."

The blood in her brain froze, her limbs in quick succession. He'd voiced her concern—that something would get in the way of the proposal as it had since the beginning. But this time it was *her*.

Her lack of credentials. *Her* lack of follow-through when it came to getting her medical license.

Something else bothered her. Reese hadn't chimed in and offered to be the physician on site.

Of course not. His life is here, and you've known that all along.

Her bottom lip trembled and before she knew it, she was crying, though no sound came from her. Just a gentle racking of her body as it processed the past two weeks. Two years. Two decades, really.

Reese let her cry it out without asking her to stop, or trying to calm her. He looked on the verge of his own breakdown, and as much as she wished she could comfort him, she didn't have anything in her.

Nothing was left.

"Hector survived, though," she finally said. He nodded his agreement and moved to her side, taking her in his arms. It was almost too much, to have his care when she was crawling out of her own skin.

"You did everything right. He would have died if you didn't act and that's not the issue. These are just suits—" He wiped at her cheeks, and smiled. She knew he was recalling what she'd called him when they first met, but she couldn't find it funny. Nothing was funny or even okay. He sobered up. "These guys are just paper pushers that want to cover their own asses and mitigate unnecessary risk."

"Ha! Unnecessary risk?" she asked. As if anything she did was for herself. She'd spent the past few decades doing whatever was asked of her because *that was the job.* Even the clinic proposal wasn't for her. It was for the community, for her father.

She screamed into a pillow. She couldn't be back from the worst week of her career, fighting not just for her life, but two others, only to have her dream killed all because she didn't have an MD next to her email signature.

"Erin, this is awful, but I'm here to help argue why they need to follow through with this. It isn't over yet."

"And who are we going to get to sign off on moving to the middle of nowhere so the board is happy?" she asked. He squeezed her tight, even though it didn't fix a damn thing, even though he didn't say the words she longed to hear—*I will.* She didn't want it for the clinic, either, but selfishly for herself. She wouldn't hear them, though, and she'd known that all along. He wasn't the same as her mom or ex-fiancé, since he lived in the city already. But he was similar in that he didn't want that kind of life for himself.

She gazed up at him and finally their eyes met. There was a rope that had been keeping her from lifting off and letting herself go. All the pressure of her job, her father, her choices… All the losses and no gains to speak of…

They'd all come with sharp instruments that threatened to undo the tether. None had come close until now. But with the quiet "snip" of an invisible cord, she let go of whatever tied her to her plans, her future, her world.

She let go and just cried.

And there was nothing Reese—or anyone else—could do to help her.

CHAPTER TWELVE

Reese was a mess. His foot tapped out a beat of regret on the linoleum flooring outside the conference room where the board was convened. They'd cleared Erin and Reese of any wrongdoing with Hector's care, but the issue remained—according to the board, at least.

They needed a physician to sign on to the project for it to move forward; without staff, it was just a good idea. *He was a physician*, four unspoken words Erin hadn't said, but that hung between them, unable to be ignored.

When she'd gone to bed in tears the night before, it had cracked his chest in two and stomped on his heart. He wanted to fix it, to make it right, or burn the world in her stead, but he froze.

Trauma response for sure, his brain offered.

Nah. That's love; you just want to make sure you get it right for her and you. His heart sounded so confident about its assessment. But how could it be love if he didn't choose her? If he hadn't gone to her to fix things?

She'd asked for a break from the routine they'd

established, but that wasn't helping anything except his anxiety. It was tightly wrapped in not having seen Erin today. His skin itched to touch hers. His lips craved hers. His arms felt empty without her in them.

Yeah, see? Love.

Trauma.

He silenced both organs.

It didn't matter why he felt the way he did, just that he did. He missed her and needed to know she was okay.

He paced the floor of the hallway until he'd earned a look of frustration from the administrative assistant who was stationed outside the conference rooms.

"The echo of shoes on this floor travels," she said. He apologized and sat back down, but then became even more anxious.

He couldn't just sit there. He had a plan—one he'd had a week ago, but hadn't wanted to put into motion without Erin's consent.

He read over the paperwork in his hand, outlining the ways the clinic was a good idea—not just for the community of Hoodsport and the outdoor visitors to the Olympic Range, but the hospital as well. They were more open to grants and tax breaks with a rural satellite campus.

The back page of the packet was more dire. What needed to happen first, or the clinic was dead in the water.

Who was going to take on the responsibility

for the clinic and the cases that required a physician? From a liability standpoint, it made sense that they'd need this in place to keep the hospital safe from litigation. He got it, academically, at least.

Personally, it was a different story.

He'd wanted to shout that he'd be the one to take the lead at the clinic, but he'd hesitated on the phone. He'd told himself it was because he wasn't the right person for the job—what would a pediatric surgeon be able to offer a remote outpost clinic that saw primarily injured hikers and outdoor adventurers?

But the truth was more complicated. He'd hedged his feelings for Erin, despite sharing a week of absolute safety and calm and pure freaking pleasure. They'd been a family, had shown they could work—in his world, at least.

What if it wasn't the same in Hoodsport, without the distraction of restaurants and walks through the city? What if Libby hated it?

He could have talked to Erin about this, but what could he say that didn't sound like an excuse?

You're a coward. Maybe, but until he knew what he could—and needed—to say, it was better to remain quiet and work to help her convince the board of the viability of her proposal regardless of the person or title attached to the project.

That's not what I mean. You don't want her project to succeed because then she will be in Hoodsport full-time and you'll have to make a choice. Go with her or let her go.

He wrung his hands and checked the time, as if it might speed up so he didn't have to follow that line of questioning. No such luck.

Damn. Was that it? Had he had the opportunity to help her get the immediate go-ahead and squandered it because he was afraid to lose her?

It didn't matter—whatever the reason, he'd missed his chance. And he'd seen what his silence did to her. He could have supported her dream by putting his name on it for now—and worked like hell to find a physician that fit the bill later. But his subconscious was right—he'd been a coward.

He'd make up for it in today's meeting, though. He had an ace up his sleeve that should help things along.

Would it make up for hurting Erin? He didn't think it would, but helping her with her dreams was a start. The thing was…even that last thought was complicated. It wasn't that he didn't want her dreams to come true so he could get what he wanted. Which, he thought might be her. No, he also wasn't convinced that the clinic was her dream, at least not fully.

He'd seen her face light up when she talked about reading *The New England Journal of Medicine.* When she'd mentioned medical school, her whole body had come alive. But when she was questioned about her plans to try and go for it, she'd shrunk almost visibly. The light had dimmed and her shoulders slumped.

He wasn't the only one hedging.

So talk to her about that. That was the plan, but he hadn't seen her. Well, he had time to kill now. Might as well have a backup plan if he needed it.

If *she* needed it.

It didn't take him long to find the number in his phone.

His old mentor from the University of Washington, Drew Johnson, answered on the first ring.

"You finally gonna relent and start giving money to the foundation?" Drew said in lieu of "hi."

"Not a chance. You have too much of my money already," Reese replied. "Or don't you look up when you head in and see my sister's name on your building?" He'd purchased the medical research wing in his sister's name in order to sustain their trauma work after Allie died.

"Touché. So why the call, then? I know you're not ready to challenge me to another golf game."

No, Reese wasn't, but he wouldn't tell Drew why that was. He didn't find golf—or tennis, or weights—exciting at all anymore. Call him crazy, but he might just take up hiking. Only in areas that weren't too far off the beaten path, of course, but he realized he'd been living a life that was too sterile, too safe, for too long.

"I wouldn't dream of it. You can keep that title for now. No, listen, Drew. I need a favor from you."

"Of course. Lay it on me."

Reese appreciated that about his mentor. He could joke with the best of them, but when push came to shove, he got down to business and was in your corner with every resource he could muster.

"It's for my—" he paused. Who was Erin to him? Girlfriend sounded so trivial compared to what she meant to him. "My partner," he finally said. It would do until he figured out how to help her. Then he'd find a way to keep her in his life.

"Tell me more. How can I help her?"

Reese explained the issue and Erin's goals once upon a time—and what had happened to bring them to the surface again. He spared no detail about the crash, the clinic, the amazing work Erin was capable of, and about her past and why medical school had been off the table for as long as it was.

"Damn. I saw that in the news. I can't believe that was you, Reese. You doing okay?"

"As well as can be expected, also thanks to Erin. Without her, we'd all be dead."

Saying that out loud, and hearing Erin's cries from the other night when she'd finally let go of all of her fear about that week in the mountains, showed him the way that was clear. She was everything. Not just in keeping them safe.

But to him. Period.

"That's intense, my man. Okay, before I roll out the red carpet, are you sure this is something she really wants? It's a huge commitment and not one to be taken lightly. Even people who have been chasing the *D-R* their whole lives don't always know what it will take to get it."

Reese understood. Erin wouldn't falter at all

under the academic aspect of the program, that he knew by watching her work on her patients, but that wasn't the only thing to consider.

Joining a medical program would mean leaving the life she'd built behind, the building of the clinic included—for now, anyway. She wouldn't be able to keep her job as an EMT—at least not that far away. Maybe she could transfer to another program?

"I'll make sure and get back to you by the end of the week. Is that okay?" Reese said. He'd talk to Erin as soon as he could.

"No rush. I'll be here, and it's not even early enrollment until next month. Thanks for calling, buddy, and I'm glad you're safe. Take care."

"You, too," Reese said, hanging up just as the door to the conference room opened.

"They're ready for you."

Erin walked up at that moment. Had she been waiting around the corner? Had she heard his conversation? She didn't give any indication she had.

"We'll be right in," he said. To Erin, he held out a hand. "Can I talk to you real quick?"

She glanced at the door, then the floor—anywhere but meeting his gaze. It killed him. Just two days ago, they'd held each other's gazes while they made love. Holy hell, he missed her.

"They're waiting on you and I. I can do it by myself if this is too much—"

"No," he interrupted. He went to take her hand, but she flinched. "That's not what I wanted to say.

I wanted to tell you I did some research last night and there's a contingency we may be able to use."

She finally looked up and met his gaze. Her eyes were red-rimmed, as if she'd been crying. All he wanted was to comfort her, but it wasn't his place. He'd caused some of this hurt and until he helped fix it, he didn't deserve her arms around him.

"I'm listening," she said. Hope lined her voice.

"We can get this ball rolling like they did in two other places with similar issues. Vancouver Island has a setup like the one you're proposing and it's backed by Vancouver Royal Hospital on the mainland. The head medic was a nurse practitioner working on her surgical degree while the clinic was built."

"I included that hospital in my literature review. I didn't know she got her surgical degree, though. That's interesting. But applying to medical school isn't easy, Reese. It's not like a quick application for a grocery rewards card—it takes time and effort, and this proposal is under fire now."

He paused, unsure if now was the time to bring up the rest of it. She was right, of course. But she was also hedging again. Keeping her dreams at arm's length. Why?

"I can help with that. I—"

"No, please stop. That's not possible. Thank you for thinking of me, but I have to do that part on my own." Her voice broke. "Let's get in there and see what they say, okay?"

He nodded. Had he said something wrong? He'd

meant to offer her a lifeline, a way to get her clinic funded and see her pursue what she really wanted, but had he screwed up and gone too far into nudging her where she hadn't wanted to go? Moreover, had his motivations been selfish since he wanted her to stay in Seattle longer? Maybe in the hopes that someone else would run the clinic by then and she'd want both him and his way of life?

No. If it was, he'd take himself out of the running as the hospital's liaison in this. Ultimately, he wanted her success, that was it.

And…his subconscious pushed.

He wanted her, too. Yeah. He wouldn't deny it.

"Sure. Can I take you out afterward to celebrate or commiserate? Libby would like to see you, too."

She shook her head. "I don't think that's wise. If I'm back in Hoodsport, I won't be able to break away to see her and I don't want her to feel like another person left her behind. I need to figure out my life, and you've got yours here."

She wasn't wrong. This had proven once and for all that their lives were on divergent paths. But they didn't have to be. Maybe… Maybe he was just being stubborn.

He'd have to examine that tomorrow, after the board meeting.

His night had been sleepless and he woke frustrated. The faces of the board members were stoic, unfeeling—the opposite of what medicine should be. There were already so many barriers to care in the US. Facing red tape and inertia from the hospital systems in place was untenable.

"Come on in and sit down. We have a full day of testimony, it seems," the president said. She met Reese's gaze and he resisted the smile that wanted to bloom. Yeah, they did. He'd called in reinforcements that could help their case for why this clinic was not only a good idea, but also necessary.

Erin fidgeted in her seat and all he wanted to do was tell the board to shove off and go to her. Reese's jaw was set, his fists clenched. So much for the beacon of calm that he always tried to be.

"Shall we get started?" the president asked. They all nodded. For the first time, Reese was nervous. If this went her way, he'd lose her to Hoodsport forever. If it didn't, she'd lose her dreams, one of them, anyway. Neither outcome sounded good, especially if she was still resisting medical school. "Can you start by introducing yourselves and this project?"

What a colossal waste of time. Still, they played nice and Erin did a magnificent job articulating the need in her rural community.

"Thank you. Can you also share the events that led to your most recent rescue attempt?"

Reese's blood went from simmer to boil in no time flat. It wasn't a "rescue attempt." It was a rescue, plain and simple. But, yeah, he understood that their crash led to another team having to rescue them. Still…without Erin's sharp, quick thinking, Hector would be dead.

"We crashed in the eastern side of the Olympic

Range, ten miles from the nearest forest service road, as we discovered. We'd medically assisted two other hikers that day and were en route home when the helicopter came across unexpected weather. We lost altitude and crashed. There wasn't time to wait for a more experienced medical professional."

"Yes," a member of the board said. Her name tag read Janet. "That opens up another line of questioning we garnered from the other three involved."

Involved? He'd asked two witnesses to come give personal testimony. Who else had chimed in?

"Which is?" he asked, earning him the same pointed look from Erin and Janet. The only difference was the meaning behind each. "Because we're here for the same reason you are—to ascertain how to best help patients. No one is on trial here."

Erin sighed. She seemed to be asking him to calm down, to play the game.

He wanted to, but it was her career on the line. How could he be cavalier with that? How could *she*?

Janet ignored his last statement.

"When you made the proposal, whom did you see running it? There aren't real doctors attached to your project at the moment. Your job description does not include surgical procedures nor full immersion in the park to rescue climbers."

Was it actually in her job description to keep searching for help in the backcountry—alone—when a patient was injured back at camp? He wished he knew more about what she did, but the reality shed a light on one glaring issue that had nothing to do with the proposal for the clinic…

Erin and Reese barely knew anything about one another. He wanted to fix that, but her walls were up now.

He half wanted to ask the board members if they would have waited for an "actual doctor" to save them in the mountains, or if they'd have been happy a competent medical professional had been there. He didn't think so. They'd be grateful, period. Besides that, Erin had shown him how amazing frontline people like EMTs were, and how vital to patient care.

"I assumed there would be support from the hospital to fill the positions," Erin said. And she was right—there should be. It wasn't up to her to fill them. She'd shown the need and it was their job to make the calls for medical professionals as needed if—when—the project was approved.

He squeezed her hand and chimed in. "I think we can all agree we need to follow protocol in this. I also think it's not a binary issue. I believe it's time to bring in the witnesses I spoke with that can represent the community in discussion."

"Well enough." The president waved her hand and the conference doors opened again. The two patients—Hector and the climber he'd medevaced out of the range—were brought in, Hector still using a wheelchair. He winked at them, and at this point, Reese couldn't keep the smile from his face.

"You did this?" she asked. It was the first time

he'd heard hope in her voice. He nodded and took her hand. This time, she let him. "Thank you."

The energy in the room changed almost instantly. It continued to grow more optimistic in favor of the clinic as the witnesses expressed the harrowing ordeal they'd been through with the flights and lack of access to closer care.

"Don't get me wrong," Hector said. "Erin saved my life. But I wouldn't have been in that position if we had a clinic that could have taken us safely on our side of the range."

"Neither would I," the climber chimed in from back in her seat.

"You can fund or not fund this clinic, but I hope you look me and every other patient in the face if you turn it down, knowing you could have saved our lives and quality of life."

It wasn't just a damn good, responsible answer, it was the truth. Erin's face said she agreed and that the testimony was just what she'd needed.

"Hmm," the board president said. Her look was unreadable, no matter how touching the speeches had been.

It was killing him to see Erin's proposal questioned in a public forum…especially because if she had the one thing she wanted—an MD beside her name—none of this would be happening. There had to be a way to get her that, at least.

"I'm sorry," he whispered. "I tried." She nodded.

"It's okay," she whispered in response. "I know."

The witnesses were shown out and the president faced Erin and Reese.

"Our last questions are about you and Ms. Wallace. Do you two have a personal relationship outside the parameters of the project you're working on together?"

"Can I ask what that has to do with anything we're discussing?" Nerves flapped in his chest like herons in flight. "Once again, this isn't a trial. We're here to talk about the clinic, not my ties to the woman whose brilliant idea it was."

"We are just concerned about your ability to be impartial here, especially with respect to a very expensive clinic proposal like this. You're the principal representative on this project for the hospital, right?"

Were they threatening her clinic? Because he and Erin had sought solace in one another during a crisis?

It was unconscionable.

"I don't see how that has anything to do with the clinic. The numbers speak for themselves. Nothing we did to stay sane interrupted my or Erin's integrity with this site visit."

It had everything to do with his life, though. Because his feelings for Erin weren't just comfort for the sake of getting over a trauma. He liked her so much more for so many more reasons.

Not that they were reasons he'd share with the inquisition that had shown up and thrown a wrench in the project. His nerves were on edge, but at least he had a backup plan in place. If the clinic bombed, at least she could get her degree and start the process over. Maybe by then, a new board would be in place. Would her feelings for him be enough if they kept this going through that process?

Is she enough? you mean. Maybe. He thought she was, but she needed to believe it, too. If she was going after her dream of medical school, maybe that would help… That could be his help—supporting that adventure for her.

"I'm sorry this is happening to you." He reached for her hand while the board murmured to one another. They linked pinkie fingers under the table and even that small contact shot straight to his heart. He really did love this woman. He knew that now. Not what it meant to his future, but the feelings were real.

"Thanks," she said. "For everything. No matter how they decide today, I'm so grateful you brought them here and that you believe in this project. If it fails, it won't have anything to do with us not trying. I'm so grateful."

He squeezed her hand. "If it doesn't go our way, will you think more seriously about whether you'd be interested in going back for your medical degree? You're an amazing EMT and I can't tell you how special it is watching you work. It's also crazy not to follow your dreams especially when I have the house that's close to campus. I know you don't want help, but I know a guy in charge up there. He says—"

"*He* says?" she hissed. "You already talked to someone about me when I asked you to let me do this alone?"

He was about to respond that, of course, he did. He wanted her to see that he'd do anything he could to help in any way he could, including reaching out to people who could support her chasing her dreams. But the doors opened and the three doctors who'd saved their asses on the mountain walked in.

"What the…?" he said. *The three people...of course.* As they settled in, Reese was more than a little curious about whether the guys were there to save them a second time—or damn them.

As the doors shut on what might be the last time before a verdict on the viability of the clinic was reached, Reese squeezed Erin's hand again.

He had to believe they'd gone through everything for a reason, and that it wasn't so they could lose everything they'd come to love.

Or what was the point?

CHAPTER THIRTEEN

ERIN DIDN'T KNOW what to think. In the span of a few minutes, the pressure she'd endured—they'd endured—for days…had dissipated. Just like that.

Well, not just like that, but still… She watched the magic that came from having not only the two patients she'd helped, but also three high-powered doctors give both medical and experienced backpacking testimony highlighting why her idea for a clinic was both sound and necessary. Her credibility might not mean a thing… But if the five of them—six, if she counted Reese, which she did—could help the board see the clinic was a good idea, she'd worry about the misogyny later.

Obviously, there was still a lingering cloud over her for not having the forethought to have gotten her medical license when she'd first wanted to, thus saving herself this drama. Not to mention the guilt at continuing to live for other people, including her father. She'd have to wrestle with that the rest of her life, if she didn't do something about it.

But, ostensibly, the talk about the clinic had shifted focus to a positive light. It was a good sign, one she would be grateful to them for—one of many things, actually. The question remained, however—how had the three docs heard about the board meeting?

"How did they know about this?" she asked Reese as Greg, Ian, and Ethan brought out a folder of data similar to what Reese had dug up about the clinic on Vancouver Island, with examples of what they'd attempted on the east coast. It all lent support to the clinic.

Her bet was that Reese had called them since he seemed bent on fixing other areas of her life as well. Not that she could fault him for his own forethought in inviting witnesses. That had been instrumental in getting them to this point—where it looked as if the clinic would pass muster.

She just couldn't put all her hopes into Reese's basket.

Why not? You care so deeply about him and he obviously cares about you.

Those two points were true, but they also failed to include one pivotal detail about Reese. He lived in Seattle and had made no expression of desire to move to Hoodsport, and why would he? He had a big, beautiful life in Seattle with restaurants, walks through the city, and cultural activities to keep his evenings full for years.

What did she have to offer him? Danger and a very pretty forest. Not enough, as it turned out. He hadn't even put his name out there for a physician that would be in charge of the clinic, even on paper.

So letting him and his choices dictate her own was off the table if she wanted to continue protecting her heart.

Do you? Really? Where has that gotten you? She ignored her heart, since it clearly didn't have her best interests in mind.

He shrugged. "I honestly don't know."

As it turned out, the three docs had heard what was happening from Hector when they'd called to check on him. He'd shared Reese's request to testify so they'd flown back to add support for the proposal on Erin and Reese's behalf.

They'd brought satellite images, indicating the crash site's remoteness and how the only reason the helicopter was there was because of the transport. With a clinic, that whole mess would have been avoided since the original injury site Hector had landed in to rescue the climber was close to the proposed clinic site. Had it been there, they'd have missed the whole Olympic Range and saved over two hundred thousand dollars.

Reese squeezed her hand, and she squeezed back. She needed to remember this had happened to him, too. But he wasn't in danger of losing his dreams, not really. At the end of the day, he would go home to his perfect city life with his small family and his medical practice, and she'd go home to...what?

Damn him for making her want *more*. In every sense of the word. From her job, her home...her love life.

"That's good, but we've got some bad press around this right now. How do we combat that? Do any of you have ideas there? The grants and things Dr. Vallen mentioned are great, but we're operating in a media deficit there, too."

Reese stood back up.

"What are you doing?" she hissed. "We're the bad press she mentioned."

"Helping them help you. Help *us*, I mean—I've already got this covered but was saving it just in case."

It was heady hearing him use that word—*us*—so cavalierly. But she didn't need saving. She needed an equal partner.

"If I may address that with the board," he said. The president nodded. "Erin Wallace used an innovative technique to save a patient's life and made the health-care field proud. To be honest, I've never seen anything like it, and with her permission, I want to cowrite an article about it for *The New England Journal of Medicine*. There are a lot of trauma docs with years of experience that are living in a box she could help them see out of, some of them here at Seattle M. We should all be so dedicated to our patients." She was speechless as he turned back to face her. She'd craved partnership, and he was offering it, at least in this capacity. Watching him mesmerize the board was intoxicating. If only he was willing to give more. "I'll give you the author credit since we clearly have a lot to learn from you."

Greg stood up next.

"And I'd like to feature it at the cardiothoracic convention next month. Would it be okay if I used the technique, Erin? And mentioned the paper you're writing, Reese?" Greg asked.

She nodded. "Of course. I'm—I'm honored. Thank you both." She'd been reading *The New England Journal of Medicine* since she was a kid and found three copies of it in the library in Port Angeles. To have her name in there would be part of a dream come true. To work on this with Reese? It was perfect—everything she didn't know she'd always wanted. "For everything."

And yet…

While it felt good—amazing, actually—to have these four men come to her side and defense in her time of desperate need, it also reminded her she was riding the current and someone else was paddling.

She needed to get out of there, but this was her show.

My show without my voice.

She was frozen to her seat, paralyzed by other people's interpretations of her dream and its viability.

"Is this enough good press for Seattle Memorial?" Reese asked.

His easy confidence was as inspiring as it was jealousy-inducing. She wished she had half his assuredness. If this clinic went through, she was going to stop being afraid of her own dreams. She deserved what he'd earned for himself. She believed that now, in part because she'd seen him not only grow himself, but also believe in her along the way. His kind of care gave her wings, even if romantically they were headed in different directions.

The board president was quiet, giving Greg the floor back.

"We're not done, either," Greg said.

"How's that?" the president asked.

"For what it's worth, we showed up today instead of calling into the meeting because two of us are investing in the clinic and are prepared to move this month to get it up and running. That's how much we believe in what Erin Wallace is doing there."

She gasped. This solved the problem the board had presented, the one problem Reese wasn't prepared to take on. "You are?"

Reese believed in her, but no one had ever believed in what she was doing enough to move to Hoodsport. Most of her people ended up making the switch out of it.

"We are. If that's something that might work for your vision of it."

She laughed. "Um, yeah."

"And provided the board relents on that and approves the clinic proposal." The board president glanced at her team, but they didn't answer right away.

The one she'd hoped might consider a move—part-time, at least—was quiet. His hand rested on hers, but…nothing. She gave him a glance.

Reese's eyes looked as if they were going to pop from his head. "Wow," he began. "That's huge."

It was, indeed.

It made her think about her own belief in what she was doing. She wanted this clinic, the town needed it, as did her father, but what did she have to offer it when she wasn't a physician? Would Reese consider moving out there and practicing as well, or would he feel stifled?

More importantly, why was everyone so sure about something as risky as upending their lives, *except* her and Reese?

People moved every day. Sure, they did, but could he? Hoodsport was amazing and he'd liked hiking—before the crash, of course—but was it enough? Was *she* enough?

Ian laughed. "Well, yeah. My brother hasn't always had the best timing or delivery skills for important conversations, but we'd hoped to talk to you about it after this—" he looked at the board "—circus."

"What would that mean? Which two of you?"

"I can't come yet, Erin," Ethan said. "I'm sorry, but I've got a parent at home that is going through long-term health issues. But I'm available for consultation anytime you need me."

"Please take care of yourself and your family. Just the offer alone is amazing." An offer Reese hadn't made even though they'd talked about what might keep them in the same place if they were open-minded and creative about their approach.

Maybe she'd misread his interest in anything long-term. She hoped not. Watching him today had reaffirmed her feelings for him and invigorated her passion for what she wanted in life, risks included.

"Are we done here?" Reese asked. "It seems as if we've proven beyond a shadow of doubt that Erin's proposal deserves a chance to change lives on behalf of Seattle Memorial."

The president glanced at the others, who nodded. Reese had done it again, swooping in to save the day.

"We'll write up the final report and get the ball rolling with these new doctors. Good luck to all of you."

The trio of doctors whooped and celebrated with high fives and fist bumps as the team filed out.

"That was badass," Ian said.

"Putting suits to bed with a warm bottle and bedtime story always makes me feel better," Greg said. Reese bristled beside her. She'd called him a suit when they'd first met, but he didn't still harbor any feelings about it, did he? He'd earned his stripes, and then some. "Whiskey, anyone?"

"Hells yes," Ethan said.

"I'm in," Ian added. They looked to Reese, who shook his head.

"Sorry, I've uh, got some things to handle that I put off for this meeting, but thanks. You guys really saved the day. I'm unbelievably grateful."

"You did more than your part, Reese. Anytime."

Reese gazed down at her, but she couldn't read

the question in his eyes. He'd was suddenly closed off in a way he hadn't been earlier. All she could figure was that his jealousy had cropped up again. Couldn't he see that *he* was the man she wanted, if he would just figure out how to talk to her, to bridge the Olympic-Range-sized gap between them?

"Erin, you go and I'll catch up with you at home later." He kissed her cheek and left her wondering what he was thinking. The word *home* stuck with her. He was her home—that much was obvious to her. Even if it didn't work out between them, he would always hold a place in her heart.

Maybe it was time to define what they were. Or end it.

That didn't sit well with her, but neither did the other option. Not with so many other things on her plate.

Ian turned to her. "You guys are badass, and we're serious about the clinic. We had a come-to-religion moment that what we're doing isn't working and there's a reason. We haven't felt that alive in a long time, not even on our weeklong adventures to cool places. Turns out we found our calling through yours, Erin. If it's wanted, that is. We don't want to encroach—like we said, there has been talk about doing the same thing back East, but there is something about this place that's calling to us."

She felt tears coming but held them back. If they fell now, they'd never stop.

"It's more than wanted. It's needed. Thank you."

"Chat about it over a drink?" Ethan asked.

She shook her head. "Would you believe I haven't been home to Hoodsport since this whole thing happened? I need to check in on my dad and Lila at the office and let her know about the clinic. Rain check? It sounds like we have a lot to talk about."

But first, she had to square things with Reese. She wasn't his thing to fix, his problem to solve. She needed partnership in all ways, not just work.

If she could just figure out what that looked like.

She hugged Greg, Ian, and Ethan, and went to find Reese. She didn't need to go far, as fate had it. She found him pacing by the window overlooking the parking lot. For a place situated in so much beauty, the city had its lion's share of concrete human impact, too.

"That went better than I expected," she said. She inhaled and put a hand on the small of his back to let him know she was there. No matter how frayed the two of them were at the moment, she cared so deeply for him. "Thanks to you. You really did so much to keep us afloat today. I'm so grateful."

"Of course. I told you I believe in you, in your ideas."

He had. And now, he'd proved it with action, at least where work was concerned.

"How are you doing?"

He turned around, and only then did she get a closer look at his face. It should have been relaxed, but it wasn't. His eyes were wild, his jaw hard like stone. She'd never seen him so agitated.

"Not good. That was too close, Erin. We need

to talk about you going back to medical school. If you had—"

"Whoa, whoa. Hold on there. Slow down. Where is this coming from?"

He ran a hand through his hair. "I've been thinking about it since we were stranded, but then the past few days—not just the board meeting, but…" He was talking so fast, as if he had to get out what was on his heart or it would burst. "But also with you living here. It's felt *right*. Now that you'll have the guys to work the clinic, you could stay in Seattle and go to school. It's win-win."

She couldn't believe what she was hearing. His answer was about *him*, and *his* feelings, not hers. Not really.

"Reese, If I had gone to medical school back then, none of this would have happened because my life would look different in every way, shape, and form. And now? I've got a full plate with the clinic and my dad… I'm happy. My life may not have the creature comforts yours does, but it is a full life. A life you've been clear you don't want for yourself. And I've been clear I don't want a life in the city."

He took her hand and she could feel the wild energy coming from him. He was always so calm, so measured. Now, he was chaos and stormy.

"Are you happy, Erin?" He ignored her statement about her life not being something he wanted. "Because I saw you out there and you loved doing that kind of medicine. You loved being in the action and you were good at it, no matter what some suits had to say about it." She was good at that, and she did love it, but she could do that in Hoodsport as an EMT, she'd shown that, especially now that they had physicians in line to run the clinic. "Why won't you invest in yourself and let me help you do that?"

She couldn't breathe in her tight, button-up shirt he'd bought her for the investigation. She undid a button around her neck, but it didn't do anything to help. It was that word—*invest*. She'd never taken herself seriously enough to consider her education in that way.

"Stop. I can't do this right now. Everything is too new, too heavy. I haven't even been home yet, for crying out loud." His mouth opened like he was going to add one more thing, but—thankfully—he thought better of it. She let go of his hand and it fell to his side like a toddler's discarded toy. "I'm going to cool off for a second. Then, will you take me back to your place?"

He winced at that last statement. She'd been calling it "home" since they'd been shacking for the past week. But it wasn't her house, not really. It was time she remembered that.

"Yeah. Sure."

Erin couldn't afford to feel bad for saying how she felt. It wasn't Reese's place to decide that, either. She had a lot to figure out and it would be better to do that alone, without him there to distract her from what was true. Namely, that she needed to go home to Hoodsport.

The drive home was quiet at first. It wasn't as

comfortable as the silences they'd shared at the end of their nights at his house. Tension filled the car.

"Tell me what you're thinking," he asked. "I want this to be you and I against the problem, not you and I against each other."

She gazed out the window, unsure how to share what she wasn't sure of herself.

"Honestly? I feel like my feet are lead, and my head and heart are drifting." It was the best way to describe it. She took a drink from the bottle of water and frowned. She missed the stream water they'd survived on.

She missed the time at the mountain, period. Missed Reese in that way… In that space. Seattle was lovely but she could never live here full-time.

"Drifting away from me?" he asked. That was the million-dollar question.

"I don't know," she whispered. "It was amazing watching you in there, and what you did for me—the patient testimony and offering me partnership with that paper."

"But?" he asked. She shook her head.

"Not *but*. And. *And* I want more. We met because I am in Hoodsport trying to get this project off the ground. It is, so I'm there."

"You weren't there because of that. You were there for reasons that aren't true anymore. And your goal is met. Why are you hiding from your real dreams? From the possibilities between us?"

She barked out a laugh that wasn't born of any type of humor.

"I'm not. It's been mere *minutes* since we made it off the mountain, Reese. In terms of time to process anything. And I went right into *your* routine—your comforts, your restaurants, your life."

"I thought we had a good time," he said. He sounded so disappointed. All she wanted was to lean into him, to find comfort in his arms as she had so many times before. Instead, she leaned against the door, the cool glass chilling her flushed face.

"We did. And we never talked about it being permanent. Would you ever consider leaving here? Being in my world?"

His jaw tightened.

"I don't know." His hands gripped the wheel tighter. "I have Libby to think about. And if you choose to go to medical school, there aren't schools in Hoodsport."

That was his answer to all of this—pushing her to something she wasn't sure how to go about.

"That wasn't my question, Reese. But I think I got my answer. Even if you came, you'd probably leave like everybody else."

He didn't say anything at first and her heart ached with the quiet.

"I want to say yes, Erin. But—" There was that word again. *But*. "I don't know what that looks like, to be honest. After Allie died, I shut that possibility off. It doesn't mean I don't care about you, though."

"I understand." She didn't, though. Not really.

How many people were like the board president—tied to a life that was easy instead of what could bring them joy if they just allowed themselves to sit in discomfort? She saved people every day who were brave enough to face their fears and venture out into the unknown. Sure, it was scary, but the alternative—a life without passion or joy, or pure wonder?

No, thank you.

Reese *had* changed, though. She could see the evidence in how he carried himself, how he claimed his space and spoke with so much earned confidence. It looked good on him, like it did on most people. It hadn't been enough time to make him want a change in lifestyle, but she couldn't begrudge him that, could she?

Some people would never know that, and it was their loss.

Ahem, her heart whispered. *You know this applies to other kinds of risks, too, right? You go out into the woods, sure, but do you let anyone into the dark forest of your heart? Are you willing to let someone love you, to really see you, or will you keep hiding in the woods?*

She mulled that over for a beat too long. She'd thought she'd let Reese in, but had she, really?

They'd walked together, cooked together, and made the kind of love she'd always dreamed about. They were, on the outside, living life side by side, at least the past week.

But she wasn't facing down any of the bigger

questions that plagued her, and in fact, hadn't even posed them to Reese for fear he'd see her and she'd be forced to confront them.

The questions wouldn't be silent now. Damn them, and him for awakening her heart and letting it ask for more.

"Do you think you're open to a relationship either way, or are you hedging because this scares you like it does me?" It was as if he'd heard inside her most private thoughts. "I mean, are you willing to take a risk when it comes to us? For—"

Was he going to say "love"?

"I think I want one with you." It was as true an answer as she could give. "Is that enough for either of us to take that risk?"

He sighed. "If I say 'I don't know' again, I'll feel like such a damned cliché. Can we eat with Libby, then talk later? I want to dig into this, but it feels like we're going in circles right now."

"Sure. But at some point, I have to go back home, Reese."

"Home," he repeated, as he stopped the car, got out, and walked over to open her door. Was he referring to hers or his? In that moment, it was clear how the two were as different as they could be.

The questions returned while Libby recounted the past two days and Erin packed.

Now that the clinic is a go, what comes next for work?

If my father doesn't need me for his care, what comes next for me?

The biggest question took up all the space in the room, and wedged itself right between her and Reese, who watched her pack with a pained expression on his face.

What role will I allow Reese to play while I search for what I want my life to look like when I get back to Hoodsport? She couldn't even define what Reese was to her.

So, no, she hadn't let him in at all, had she? And if she wasn't going to, or wasn't able to, rather… she needed to let him go.

Her heart raged against that idea.

You can't do that—you love him. Yeah, she probably did, but that wasn't enough, was it? They were too different. Their lives too disparate outside the circumstances that had thrust them together.

She gathered her things in the bathroom, then ran headlong into Reese on her way out. His solid, steady presence had made her feel so safe and cared for when they'd been stranded. And afterward, as she processed what had happened, too.

Now, though, it only served to act as a wall to keep her pinned in place. Even though she could take a step backward, or to the side to get around him, she felt trapped. This man represented everyone who'd chosen to leave her for a better life somewhere with *more*.

Would she really, after all this time, do the same to herself? Abandon all she'd worked for just for a couple letters next to her name and some good Thai food restaurants?

No. She'd be such a hypocrite if she did that.

When you get new information, it's okay to make a different choice, her conscience reminded her. Funny how it sounded a lot like Reese.

But what was new? That she wanted to go to med school? Sure. But at what cost? She'd be giving up too much.

"I can't," she whispered, speaking to the unasked question in his eyes. He tried to pull her into an embrace, but she couldn't be held, not when she wanted to explode, to come apart. It made her claustrophobic.

"Please." She shook her head. Her skin itched—whether with desire to be closer to him or to run away, she couldn't tell. Both options seemed impossible at the moment. So did sitting where she was.

"Just consider school. For you and us. We could be together and I know it's something you want, too."

"I don't know how to explain it, except that I've been riding upstream on the tides of other people's decisions for my whole life and haven't been able to swim at my own pace, to take a different fork in the river, or even get out and walk for a bit." She paused and giggled nervously. None of this was actually funny, except in a cosmic sense. "Sorry, all my analogies are water-related."

"That's why I love you, Erin," he said. He was

the one to close the gap between them, and she shivered when he took her hands in his. Her laugh evaporated in the stale air.

"You love me." It was a statement, not a question. It was heavy on her tongue, but worse out in the open. "How is that possible? You barely know me. You haven't seen my house, or met my dad. You haven't taken me out to dinner and seen how long I take with a wine menu."

His smile undid her so she looked down at her feet. She needed all her strength.

"I have taken you out to dinner and we had whiskey, remember?"

She tried to pull away—to go where, though? She was at *his* house, in *his* life. It was never more apparent that it was more than just the three hours between their homes that separated them.

"I was in triage and needed steak and whiskey, not in that order. The date part was secondary."

"You're saying the past two weeks haven't meant anything to you?"

No. That was the problem. They'd meant too much and now, it was time to go back to reality. To the life she'd built herself.

"Please tell your friend thank you but that I'm going home to build this clinic before anything else gets in the way."

She left and vowed not to look back. On the way, she called Lila and asked for a ride home. She'd take a cab to the airport and wait.

Love was as unpredictable as the weather, and

she wouldn't wait around to see whether it would leave her stranded on a beach or trapped in a cave to avoid a hailstorm.

She might drown on dry land, but at least it would be her call, her choice.

CHAPTER FOURTEEN

Reese worked from home the next three days, catching up on charts and emails he'd ignored since he got back from the "excursion" in the mountains. The hospital administration offered him another week of respite to keep healing up and get right, but he didn't take it. There was already too much waiting for him to respond to, work he'd ignored when Erin had stayed. The rigmarole of being a doctor attached to a big program was a full-time job without considering the patient care. Erin certainly had it right—minimize the distractions, concentrate on what brings you joy and pays the bills.

By the end of the third day, he had caught up, but he'd also earned a sore back and his head was a mess. Part of that was his lack of sleep. After he put Libby down, he was always exhausted, but he just couldn't get comfortable without Erin there. She felt like home, and he was restless without her.

"Eff this," he said that morning. He called his mom and asked if she could keep Libby for dinner, which she was delighted to do, as long as it wasn't for "dinner and a week of being lost in the mountains."

He'd laughed at that quip, knowing it came from a pervasive seed of worry his mother held about him, especially after they'd lost Allie. He told her he'd be back before dark, which went over well with her.

"Just a quick hike to clear my head."

"Can I ask you a quick question before you take off?"

"Yes, I have a sat phone now. And all the 'just in cases' this time. I have a first aid kit, waterproof basics, extra socks, and a utility knife, even." No way he was gonna be caught with his pants down in the wilderness again.

"I'm glad to hear it, but that's not what I wanted to check on. Libby said you asked if she'd want to visit Hoodsport soon."

He murmured something about his daughter being a chatty Kathy.

"Yeah. Just curious if she'd, you know, want to go for some hikes out there." Maybe if he could get her out young, she'd grow up with a healthy appreciation—and respect—for nature.

"You're thinking of moving," she said. He was so glad she was on the phone and not in person so she couldn't see his face. He'd barely thought about that possibility himself—how did she know? "I'm your mom," she added. "I know everything, remember?"

"I'm recalling it now. Being a teen sucked thanks

to that little party trick of yours. Allie and I were always getting caught for stuff."

She laughed. "You two were good kids. I didn't need to worry. But for what it's worth, we're both in favor of you taking that chance."

"Both? You and Dad?"

"No, Libby and I. We talked about it and think a change of pace would be good for you both."

Reese didn't know what to say to that. He wasn't moving, just…thinking about it. And his mom and daughter might as well be packing the house.

"I've got to go if I'm gonna be back for dinner."

"Sure, sweetie. We'll chat soon. Be safe and love you."

Just after noon, he headed out. He didn't know where he was going until he made it to Port Angeles. At the gas station, he looked up some of the trails at the base of the Olympics, finding he missed the fresh air and feeling of being…away from it all. They weren't too technical, but a run in the hills by Elwha River sounded perfect. He could escape the worries that seemed relentless, for a few hours at least.

Well, sort of. Every now and then a ping from his backpack warned him that the world nipped at his heels. He should turn off his notifications, but on the off chance Erin might call…he pulled out his phone every damn time.

None of them were her, though. Just emails, one from his mentor telling him he'd still do anything to help Erin if she changed her mind. He'd get back to him later.

Yeah, not likely she'd do an about-face like that. She'd made her case crystal clear. She needed agency in her own life, and while he didn't begrudge her that at all, she was pushing away things that could help her claim that just because…

Well, because no one had stayed before.

He was counted among those people, he figured. That was the worst part of all. In living where he lived, and not being willing to leave, he'd hurt her by being just like everyone else.

And in doing so, he'd lost the best thing to ever happen to him.

That's the biggest load of bullshit you've spat today.

His head was his own worst enemy these past few days, filled with shouldas, couldas, and wouldas. It was part of why he'd opened up to the "maybe" of Hoodsport.

He should've been more patient, more inquisitive about what she wanted outside being an EMT instead of telling her what program would be best for her and how to get in—with his help, of course. He could've been a better listener.

He would've been, had she not told him she needed to leave, that she wanted space and would contact him when she was ready.

Hence why he was religiously checking his phone. He'd messed up, sure, but he'd been up front about how he felt and it wasn't enough.

What more could he have done to share what was in his heart with Erin, to let her see how much he cared about her? He'd said he loved her, but that was obviously the wrong move.

The thing was, he was pretty damn sure she loved him back. But she was scared of what that meant because no one had ever come to her, had stuck around.

Halfway through the inner monologue that wouldn't let up, another ping sounded from his phone. Of course, he dug it out, but it was just another email from his mentor.

This particular subject line had him intrigued. It read, University of Washington Opens New Medical Track for Students—Opening for Letters of Interest in the New Year.

He read the email twice and smiled.

It was a fully funded grant program, inviting aspiring doctors to apply to a low-residency trauma program. They could do their three years almost entirely remote.

This is something I can help with, Drew said at the top of the email forward. He shot back a note of thanks, but that wouldn't be necessary. Erin would want to get in on her own accord. That is, if she even opened an email from Reese.

Hmm… She might not want to hear from him, but maybe the guys could be his emissaries. She'd been so right about the jealousy when it came to them, but not from a romantic standpoint. He didn't question the connection they shared, just what he could offer her. They had free access to her curiosity and support, while he had to work for both.

Yeah, because you were a suit. Give it time and show her you're not.

What did it matter?

Because you know her, and what will make her happy. The city isn't it. It never was. Your curiosity about moving is well-timed, buddy.

He paused and let the sound of the Elwha River soothe his aching heart. More than anything, he wished he could tell Erin how much she was right about one thing—life was better outside. Thankfully, he'd realized that before Libby was too much older and she could get used to her life as a partner in adventure.

He called Ian; at the least he could get this information to Erin somehow.

Something unlocked in his brain just as the other line went active.

"Reese. Good to hear from you. What's up?"

"Hey," he said. "I just forwarded you an email. Any chance you could share this with Erin? I don't think she's down to hear from me, especially since she almost left me on a mountain peak last time I brought up medical school."

"I'm looking at it right now." There was a long pause, where Reese assumed Ian was perusing the missive. "Damn. This is definitely something I could see her jumping at. It's low-residency, so she can work at the clinic as our EMT while she's going to school, then we can have her for the residency. Hmm. I'll share it for sure."

"Thanks, man."

"No worries. I'm sorry it didn't work out between you two. It'd be nice to have you on board as a pediatrics guy. That, and I know she really cares about you. She asked about you the other day, you know."

Reese hated that his heart leaped at that.

"Really?" He tried for nonchalant, but from the chuckle Ian gave him, he'd come up short of desperate.

"I'll send this to her, but maybe you oughta give her a call sometime. I'm sure she'd like to know how you and Libby are doing."

Reese assured his new friend he'd do that, and hung up.

The thing he'd been on the verge of processing before Ian had answered clicked into place.

Reese hadn't shown Erin anything, actually.

All the risk he'd thought he'd taken? Yeah, what a lame-ass excuse for making a half-hearted effort. All he'd done was present her with one option and get mad when she didn't take it.

What the actual hell was that?

Nothing he'd want an amazingly beautiful, intelligent, independent woman to take. On top of that, he'd not been willing to make the same move he was asking her to make. A daughter and a career were big challenges, sure. But not insurmountable ones. Hell, they were things people dealt with every day as they made new changes in their lives. The guys were doing it, and from the sounds of it, one of them had a kid he was bringing in tow, not much older than Libby. And Reese was only three hours away by car and he'd not even pretended he couldn't keep his place in the city so they could use it when they wanted to.

Man, he'd messed up worse than he'd thought.

Yeah, you did. What an idiot, his heart said.

Finally, his brain added. *You're getting it. The question is, what're you gonna do about it?*

He didn't know. Well, he sorta did, but it was out of his control.

At least the two organs were in unison at this point. They'd been battling since the start about the risk it took to let someone in and how devastating it would be to lose them. It turned out that it wasn't worse than not loving them at all.

That didn't change the part about Erin's agency in the whole thing. She was right on that count, too. She deserved to make the call herself. All he could do was present her with the options and hope she felt the same about him.

If not, he'd let her go. He loved her that much.

He called Ian back. "Hey, sorry, bud. I just have one more question."

"No worries. We're just chilling after getting off the plane. Turns out six round-trip visits to the west coast don't sit as well on the lumbar as they did in our twenties."

Reese laughed. Regardless of how intimidated

he'd been by the guys, he liked them. They were funny, smart as hell, and adventurous enough that he was excited to learn from them.

If they took him up on his plan.

"Is Erin still on the hiring crew for the clinic?"

"Nope. She's all but handed the hiring and construction over to us, why?"

That surprised Reese. She'd been so invested in this project that Seattle Memorial had a stack of proposal requests from her ten deep at least. And now, she'd handed it over?

"Um, well, I was hoping I could talk to you about that comment you made earlier. About needing a pediatrician on hand. Was there any meat to that, or were you just shooting the breeze?"

Ian laughed. "Man, if you were seriously open to it, I'm as serious as a heart attack. Excuse the bad analogy. But for real. Do you think you'd want to? I know Erin would be interested. She's only brought that up a dozen times in the past few days."

She had? That boded well, but until he heard it from her, he wouldn't make the move.

"That's great, but I think I'll start with pitching one day a week there and see how she is with that. I should be transparent with you… I'm in love with the woman and would like her to see that this move is serious for my career, but also show her that she matters to me deeply. If she asks me to leave because that doesn't work for her, I don't want to leave you in a lurch, but I'll have to honor that. If she asks me to stay, I'd like to know I can."

He exhaled. Whew. He'd said it all.

"I get it, and I have to say I'm thrilled for y'all. Erin's great and she clearly cares about you. I'll draw up a permanent full-time contract, as well as a provisional one, just in case. Good luck, man."

"Thanks, Ian. I appreciate it more than you know."

Reese hung up and smiled. If she didn't want him to get involved, he'd back off, but he would show her he was serious about her and let the chips fall where they may.

Since making wagers was a risky business, he'd never been a betting man. But if he wanted something he'd never had before, he had to be willing to do something he'd never done. And Erin Wallace, hero and love of his life, was worth the risk.

CHAPTER FIFTEEN

THERE WERE NO parking spaces left outside the clinic, including the one Erin usually claimed as her own. Greg and Ian were there at the conference table, of course—Lila, too—but whose car was the black all-terrain?

She walked in and was met with her answer in the finest form she'd ever seen him.

Dammit.

"What are you doing here?" she asked. He hadn't texted to let her know he was in town, but was he supposed to? She'd closed the door pretty firmly in his face the last time they'd been together.

He looked so different from that day, standing in his OR hiking pants and a zip-up fleece. He'd even let his beard grow out to a four-day stubble.

C'mon, she begged the universe, asked of her heart. *If I can't be with him, can he at least not be even more handsome? It's not fair.*

It's not us keeping you from him. You know darn good and well you can be with him if you get out of your own way. You can do a lot of things that are amazing if you get out of your own way. Like open that application to Tacoma's outdoor trauma medical program, the universe—or her own heart—whispered back.

Definitely her heart, with that kind of snark.

"Thanks a lot," Greg said. "What are we, ground elk meat?"

"Sorry. But I was expecting you two." To Reese, she said, "Nice to see you. I just didn't think I was going to."

Like, ever again.

"I'm here to consult on the pediatric program. If you all think I'm a good fit, I'll set up an outpost practice here once a week at first, then see if more is needed."

Reese's gaze never left hers. It was as if no one else existed.

"What?" she asked. "No one told me. But, um, that sounds good." As long as she didn't think about what that meant—he'd be in Hoodsport a day a week, at least. More if she thought—they thought—he was a good fit.

You are! Her heart rejoiced, but her body told it to shut the hell up. Her overeager heart was henceforth suspended from making any decisions on behalf of Erin's more responsible organs since it was the thing that had fallen for Reese—in all his unattainable glory—in the first place.

He's not the one who's unattainable. As far as I recall, you're the one who turned him down and hunkered into a safe life with no risk—not him.

She ignored her heart and hummed some punk

rock song from her teen years to drown out her protestations. He'd asked her to come to Seattle, but he hadn't laid anything on the line, either.

"Did you get the email about the trauma program?" Ian asked. She nodded. *This* was a topic she was happy to talk about.

"Thanks, yeah. I actually applied and got an early acceptance."

"Don't thank us, thank—" Greg said, earning a kick under the table, not only from Ian, his brother, but… Reese? What was that about?

"Tell us more. That's so cool, Erin."

She glanced at Reese, whose gaze was pinned to the floor. Something was off, or there was something he wasn't saying and wanted to.

She focused on Ian and Greg. "Well, the director called last night. He'd heard my story, and did his research. He said he'd actually like me to see what I can test out of, so I might only have a two-year program to complete. Either way, it's perfect since it's a hybrid program. I can live here for the education part and then come back to the clinic for the residency if you'll have me."

"You're welcome here anytime, Erin," Ian said. He'd unofficially taken on the role of chief medical officer for the clinic, but it would have been his, either way. He was the most responsible out of all of them and he had the background from his previous position. She couldn't believe they'd been lucky enough to have the two docs who rescued them join the program. It was going to be a helluva medical program.

"I second that," Greg added.

"Thanks, guys." She looked at Reese, whose gaze finally met hers.

And you? she wanted to ask. *What do you think?* Reese was consulting? That made him more an employee than she was, or would be. Until she had her license, anyway.

For the first time, she felt a measure of pride in her choice, in her future. It was hers. But it still felt like something was missing.

Yeah, him— She shut her heart up again before it could finish that thought.

"I'm so proud with and of you, Erin."

Her brain put together the pieces just a fraction too late.

Reese. He'd had a hand in this.

"Did you have something to do with this?" she asked.

He held up his hands in defense.

"No. I promise. I sent the email to Ian, but I swear, I had nothing to do with the spot you were offered. I told Drew to back off and let you have this one for yourself."

"Oh," she said. She appreciated that she could say that she'd gotten in herself. "Thanks."

"Of course. If you want to talk about anything related to class stuff, though, I hope you consider me. I'd love to still support you, Erin."

Why did he have to look so good while he sat in her clinic, wanting and missing him fiercely?

She hadn't been very involved in the logistics now that the clinic was being built out. Instead, she'd thrown herself into medical rescue cases as was her role as an EMT. It was satisfying work, but that's not why she did it. She'd needed a distraction from the pull that was Reese, or medical school, or more likely both.

She'd shut the door on those both, needing space to get out of the current that had been carrying her faster and faster toward a life she hadn't chosen for herself.

But she'd been on dry land for a while now.

Looking at his curious smile framed by facial hair she itched to run her hands down, she realized how much she missed him. No amount of distance or distraction had numbed that particular need.

Unfortunately.

Which was why… No matter how little involvement she'd had in the project, she at least hoped someone—Greg and Ian, or even Lila—would have given her the heads-up that the man she couldn't forget, the man who'd changed everything, was in town. Regardless of whether he'd helped her get into school, or not, he was here. In her space.

Asking to work at *her* clinic. Well, not her clinic, but the idea was her baby, and so no matter what, even if she couldn't practice in it, she could think of it as hers.

In reality, though, she loved the name the board

had agreed to. The Hector Ruiz Medical Center. It was so fitting to honor the man who'd risked everything to fly them home safely, a man who represented why this clinic was so needed in the first place.

"I think we should do a quick survey of where the surgical suite should be set up," Ian said.

"We just did that—" Greg began. Ian sent his brother a pointed look that would have made Erin laugh if she was in a space to find this situation funny.

She'd asked Reese to give her agency and he had, but she'd scared him so much, he hadn't even felt comfortable talking to her about an opportunity that was perfectly suited to her. He'd also held back from offering any support—all thanks to her inability to be brave.

She could careen off cliffs, hike for dozens of miles in the backcountry in all weather, and save lives by making medical devices out of household items.

But she hadn't taken a real risk with the one thing she had to give—her heart. And Reese deserved that. He'd shown up for her, come to her town and offered up his services in pursuit of her dream.

Ian and Greg left, and then it was just her and Reese.

"You might work one day a week?" she asked.

"I have the paperwork ready to go, but wanted to run it by you first. This is your baby." That he could read her mind like that never ceased to impress her. They were so connected. How had she gone so long without him?

"Oh, thanks, but it's fine. Um, when?"

"I wanted to stick to days you were off so I didn't get in the way. If you need more, I can—"

She was by his side in a moment, her arms wrapped around his neck before he could say anything.

"I need more."

His gaze searched hers. "Erin, I'm here for whatever you need."

"I know," she said. "I've known all along, but was a little afraid to admit it to myself and what it might mean."

His hands lingered near her waist and she felt the kinetic energy between them. She placed his hands firmly on her skin, and for the first time in days, weeks, even, she relaxed.

"What—" he began, but she put a finger to his lips.

"No. I need to say something, then I'm going to kiss you. Is that okay?" The way his eyes lit up and the corners of his mouth turned up in a smile, told her he agreed before his soft nod.

"Yes. Can we switch the order of that?" He leaned in and kissed her nose, and she giggled. "It's just more efficient that way."

"You're such a suit, concerned with efficiency." She laughed and then kissed him softly at first.

When he deepened the kiss, she opened her mouth to receive him.

"Good thing I have a passionate woman to remind me to throw efficiency to the wind from time to time," he whispered against her lips. She nodded.

"You have me, Reese. That's all I wanted to say. My feeling about being here isn't the same without you, and if you want, I'll come to Seattle and do my classes from there. I just realized you are home. Wherever you are is where I want to be."

He smiled and hugged her tight against him.

"I was hoping you'd say that. I asked for a full-time contract to be drawn up for me to join you here, if you'll have me. I'm just a suit, but—"

"But you're my suit," she whispered, kissing him. "And, yes. I want you here. For now. We can talk about part-time in both places if you want."

Reese shook his head. "Nah. I'm happy here, with you, in this beauty. Libby picked out a dozen houses she wants to show you."

"Why?"

"Because, love, I want you to live in it with us, to make this decision together. What do you say?"

Erin didn't need to think about that for more than three seconds. "I think that sounds amazing, Reese, as long as I can ask you a favor. A question, really."

"Anything. You've just made me the happiest man alive."

"Do you love me?" she asked.

He kissed her once, then again, then a third time.

"I love you so damn much," he said. "Did you really question that?"

She shook her head, her body a ball of kinetic energy. "Not at all. I just botched it last time you told me that and didn't get a chance to tell you that I love you, too."

They kissed for who knew how long.

"I actually do have one more question," he said.

"It'd better be a good one if you're gonna stop kissing me to ask it," she said.

Reese got up, leaving her standing there, in love, her whole body on fire for this man she loved so deeply she wondered how she'd survived the past little while without him near her.

He came back with a small box and knelt in front of her. She joined him. No way were they doing anything resembling their future on uneven ground.

"Erin, I need to ask you that question."

She nodded. "The answer is yes, I think."

"Can I still ask?"

She laughed. "Of course."

"Will you please spend the rest of your life loving Libby and me?"

"Oh, that's all?" she teased.

"That's all. Oh, and I promise to love and care for, and take risks for and with you forever. How's that?"

She thought about it and decided then and there. Risk was hard when it came to her heart, but love was worth it.

"It's perfect."

EPILOGUE

"THERE'S THE WOMAN of the hour," Reese said, sliding a hand around her waist, which was decidedly larger than when they'd met three years ago. "My little incubator."

"Cute. I don't think we're keeping that nickname, though, hun. Not if you want to live to see her born." She giggled as he nuzzled her neck. "There's nothing little about me, either. Thank goodness, we're about to meet this tiny human soon. She's killing my sleep and sexy time with my husband."

Reese's low growl in her ear didn't match that last sentiment. To be honest, if anything was killing her sleep, it was the fact that, for three years now, her husband hadn't been able to keep his hands off her.

Unless she asked for time to study, and then he was all about the boundaries she'd set. It had paid off, so who was she to test his methods?

"You said, 'she'?" he asked, pulling her hair to one side and almost knocking off her graduation cap. "Did you cheat and look at the sonogram, my love?"

He bit her neck playfully, eliciting a small cry of pleasure from her.

"We're at my medical school graduation, show some decorum, Mr. Vallen."

The heat from his breath as he laughed warmed her neck…and the parts of her that perpetually wanted this man. Gosh, how had she gotten so lucky?

"I intend to do no such thing, Mrs. Vallen."

"That's Dr. Vallen to you."

"I'm so proud of you. You are going to be an amazing doctor, Erin." The honey-sweet sentiment didn't erase their playful banter; it was simply one more way the two had grown to love one another since the series of events that had brought them together.

"Thank you, love."

He nipped at her earlobe and earned a couple stares from an elderly couple to their left. Ah, let them. She was graduating medical school, married to the man of her dreams, and pregnant with their first child. They deserved to celebrate however suited them.

Don't forget the biggest part—we survived.

That they did. Except, she thought as the speakers crackled and the president of the university stood to greet the graduates, surviving wasn't the biggest obstacle they'd overcome. Finding and believing in love was the hardest thing of all.

What was easy? Greg and Ian were rolling out the clinic and doing a wonderful job at their new roles. So far, it was just what the town needed; there was even talk about bringing in a veterinarian that would help dogs that were with owners when they were stranded or hurt. The hospital had fully said no to that one, to laughter from Erin and Reese.

Ian had started a hiking club in the area, Greg was talking about going half in on a brew-pub, and even Ethan was enjoying coming to visit when his mother's treatments were going well. She'd gone into remission for two years, but last year, it had come back. Cancer was the worst, and the only downside to the guys' new move was not being able to show up for Ethan as often as they'd like.

"You two are sappy enough to sell your own maple syrup."

Erin laughed. "Hector, if that isn't the most hypocritical—"

"Careful, Doc. I'm not as strong as you. You gotta go easy on me." He still hugged her so tight, she could feel the pressure in her chest. "Congrats, Erin. You deserve this and so much more. I wouldn't be here without you and other Doc."

"I'm 'other Doc'?" Reese asked.

Hector winked at him. "Man, you two are the best thing that ever happened to me, but today is Erin's. You're second fiddle, sorry."

Reese laughed and shrugged.

"Touché. Well, I had to try."

She wiped at tears on her cheeks. Her family was so beautiful. Hector's wife waved enthusiastically from the stands, though her eyes were on the toddlers running amok. She had her hands full with the twins they'd had just a month and a half after their crash and rescue.

"You're it, Doc. You'll always be number one in the Ruiz family."

"Shhh. No going there, and no fair. I'm all hormonal. You can't say such nice things to me. Teasing only." He laughed, but hugged her again, earning her another round of tears. "If you ruin my makeup, Hector Ruiz, I will…"

"What? Name another clinic after me?" He put a hand around her shoulder and kissed the top of her head. "In all seriousness, Doc, I'll never be able to thank you enough. For all of it. Now, go make us proud, then get to work in that clinic."

He laughed, blew her a kiss, and jogged up to the stands to meet his family. He'd healed just fine. They all had.

Love was such a big part of that…

"We did a good thing, Doc," Reese said, kissing her on the lips. His love had been the most instrumental in healing her. Not only from the crash, but also from a life lived going downstream with someone else's plans for her. With Reese's care and love, she was now living the life she wanted.

She put his hand on her stomach just as the baby kicked. "That we did."

He grinned from ear to ear the way he always did when they got to feel their daughter move.

As Reese found his seat—not before snapping a few selfies of himself with her, then her belly, then the three of them—she recalled the months following the accident, where Reese had encouraged her to get back in a helicopter, in clear weather, anyway, and to explore the Pacific Northwest with him.

The way he put it, he'd come back to life loving her, and realized that they were both right—risk was an unavoidable part of life and would come barreling down the path even if it seemed like there weren't any clouds on the horizon. The trick? Pick risk you could live with, risk that promised a beautiful life if it all worked out.

Then work like hell to make it all work out.

The rest was out of their control, and that was okay.

"Erin! You did it!" a high-pitched voice screamed from the other side of the field. Erin and Reese turned to see Libby running toward them, Reese's mother and her own father close behind, smiles on all their faces. The girl had welcomed Erin in almost immediately, as had Reese's parents and siblings, which was a gift Erin didn't plan on squandering. Thankfully, Libby also seemed to be thrilled to take on the role of big sister.

That was the biggest gift of all. In meeting Reese, she'd met a man who would stand beside her and hold her hand through the hard and the risk and the unknowns life offered as part of its cost of living it. They spent half their time in Seattle, practicing at Seattle Memorial, the other half working at the clinic the two doctors from the east coast ran in her stead.

And she'd also been gifted a family with Reese. Even her father had settled into peaceful nights playing cards with the Vallens instead of mapping out his post-care adventures.

Well, instead of only planning adventures.

Because that was the crux of it; everything was better with a little risk and a little peace blended together, to make a full, balanced, beautiful life.

"Any thoughts on what you'd like to do for dinner since this is as much a celebration for you as it is for me?" she whispered to him as Libby launched into a monologue about what she'd wear to her own medical school graduation one day.

"How so?" he asked, his hand absently rubbing circles on her stomach. She hoped they'd always be this in tune with one another. "And, yes, I have. Dinner is taken care of."

"Is it, now?" She secretly loved that her partner took it upon himself to plan dates for her. After so long being in charge of everything and managing everyone else's lives, it felt good to be taken care of from time to time. "And this day is for both of us since I wouldn't have pursued this if it wasn't for your—"

"My stubbornness that you love so very much?" He handed her the program, her name at the top of page one as the student award recipient.

She used it to teasingly slap her husband on the shoulder.

"Exactly. You saw something in me I'd stopped

looking for and I can't thank you enough for unearthing it."

He smiled and kissed her, earning a squeal from Libby.

"Come on, Lib. Let's go see if they're still selling candy at the entrance," Erin's dad said. "I could use some chocolate myself."

When they'd left, Reese took Erin in his arms, her swollen belly in between them.

"You did the same for me, love," Reese said. "Thank you for being the biggest risk and best reward I've ever accomplished." That was saying a lot since the two had climbed Mount Foraker in the Denali Range together last year. She touched her belly. Almost exactly nine months earlier, actually.

She hoped their daughter, their youngest, would be a blend of the adventurous spirit that made her possible, and the hope that risk was something worth taking.

"And you're mine. You're home, Reese. All of you."

They kissed and the rest of the crowd disappeared into the periphery while she poured all her love into her husband, into her big, beautiful life.

"Any chance you've picked a delayed honeymoon location yet?" he asked her. She smiled up at her husband, a man who made good on every promise he'd ever made her.

"Anywhere that doesn't involve a tent."

He laughed loud, his head thrown back in joy—her second favorite iteration of her love.

"Fair enough. I might be able to spring for a luxury suite on a beach somewhere, if that sounds okay." His smile said he knew what she really wanted and would do anything to give it to her. Beaches were fine, but they weren't their home, their place.

"How about a cabin with a bathroom and a bed, and maybe even a kitchen up north?" They'd loved their time in Alaska and wanted time there post-baby to explore the terrain and one another.

"Done. I love you, Dr. Vallen."

"I love you, Reese. And always will."

They kissed, sealing the promise as they did dozens of times a day as they grew in love and partnership.

They might not know what was around the corner, but they had everything that mattered just then.

And that was the best payoff they could ask for. It was life, and it was beautiful.

* * * * *

Look out for the next story in
the High Altitude Docs trilogy
Coming soon!
And if you enjoyed this story, check out these
other great reads from Kristine Lynn

Doctor's Nine-Month Rival
Wedding Date with Dr. Petrides
How to Resist Your Enemy

All available now!